The worst birthday ever

Fish was looking at me expectantly. I was about to explain that I had to be the one to go wake Poppa. It was just that simple—my savvy was waking things up, just like Samson's turtle. I knew that a savvy wasn't something you could make happen for wanting, but I had proof that the means of waking up Poppa were there and wrapped up in me, ready to burst out like Rocket's sparks or Fish's wind and rain—if I could just find my way to Salina. I was about to tell my brother all of this, but at that moment Will Junior found us.

"Happy birthday, Mibs," he said, smiling. "Aren't you coming in to the party?"

"I'm coming," I said to Will, jerking my arm free from Fish's tight grip.

Fish let me go, but he gave me a look like the sharp end of a stick, and punctuated his meaning with a smattering of abrupt, uncontrolled raindrops from the clouds overhead. I gave Fish a *look* right back. Then I smiled my own smile at Will Junior and let him pull me into the church, straight into the catastrophe that was my thirteenth birthday party.

OTHER BOOKS YOU MAY ENJOY

Counting by 7s	Holly Goldberg Sloan
Fish in a Tree	Lynda Mullaly Hunt
Matilda	Roald Dahl
Scumble	Ingrid Law
Short	Holly Goldberg Sloan
Soar	Joan Bauer
Switch	Ingrid Law
Thirteen	Lauren Myracle
Twelve	Lauren Myracle
Under the Egg	Laura Marx Fitzgerald

Savvy

by Ingrid Law

PUFFIN BOOKS / WALDEN MEDIA

FOR HANNAH WITH LOVE AS YOU BLOW OUT THIRTEEN DRIPPING CANDLES

PUFFIN BOOKS
An imprint of Penguin Random House LLC
375 Hudson Street
New York, New York 10014

This book is published in partnership with Walden Media, LLC.
Walden Media and the Walden Media skipping stone logo are trademarks and registered trademarks of Walden Media, LLC, 17 New England Executive Park, Building 17, Suite 305, Burlington, Massachusetts 01803.

First published in the United States of America by Dial Books for Young Readers, a division of Penguin Young Readers Group, 2008
First published by Puffin Books, a division of Penguin Young Readers Group, 2010
This edition published by Puffin Books, an imprint of Penguin Random House LLC, 2018

THE LIBRARY OF CONGRESS HAS CATALOGED THE DIAL BOOKS
FOR YOUNG READERS EDITION AS FOLLOWS:
Law, Ingrid, date.
Savvy / by Ingrid Law.
p. cm.
Summary: Recounts the adventures of Mibs Beaumont, whose thirteenth birthday has revealed her "savvy"—a magical power unique to each member of her family—just as her father is injured in a terrible accident.
ISBN 978-0-8037-3306-0 (hc)
[1. Magic—Fiction. 2. Brothers and sisters—Fiction. 3. Voyage and travels—Fiction.] I. Title.
PZ7.L41836Sav 2008 • [Fic]—dc22 2007039814

Puffin Books ISBN 9780142414330

Designed by Teresa Dikun

Printed in the United States of America

27th Printing
BANG

Acknowledgments

With loving, heartfelt gratitude to Rick and Shirley for being my safe harbor in every big storm; to Michelle for the sustenance of books and listening and scallion pancakes; and to Sean, for always reading, always writing, and never letting me forget to "find down tiny."

Special thanks to Lauri Hornik, Regina Castillo, to the Dial/ Puffin design team, and to all of the extraordinary people at Penguin Young Readers Group; to Deborah Kovacs, Micheal Flaherty, and the wonderful group at Walden Media; and to Brandon Dorman for his incredible artistry and gorgeous storms of color. Additional thanks to Sarah Hughes at Puffin in the U.K., and to all of the other editors around the world who have welcomed *Savvy* (and to Maja Nikolic and Elena Santogade at Writers House, for helping to put the book into the hands of those editors), as well as to Kassie Evashevski at UTA, for her work on the West Coast.

Finally, for their ridiculously amazing extra-special know-how, and their nonstop support and good humor, I extend my ardent appreciation and unequivocal admiration to my agent, Daniel Lazar at Writers House, who I am convinced never sleeps, and to my editor-extraordinaire, Alisha Niehaus, who always knows when to hold my hand and when to give me a good strong push.

WHEN MY BROTHER FISH TURNED THIRTEEN, we moved to the deepest part of inland because of the hurricane and, of course, the fact that he'd caused it. I had liked living down south on the edge of land, next to the pushing-pulling waves. I had liked it with a mighty kind of liking, so moving had been hard—hard like the pavement the first time I fell off my pink two-wheeler and my palms burned like fire from all of the hurt just under the skin. But it was plain that Fish could live nowhere near or nearby or next to or close to or on or around any largish bodies of water. Water had a way of triggering my brother and making ordinary, everyday weather take a frightening turn for the worse.

Unlike any normal hurricane, Fish's birthday storm had started without warning. One minute, my brother was tearing paper from presents in our backyard near the beach; the next minute, both Fish and the afternoon sky went a funny and fearsome shade of gray. My brother gripped the edge of the picnic table as the wind kicked up around him, gaining momentum and ripping the wrapping paper out of his hands, sailing it high up into the sky with all of the balloons and streamers roiling together and disintegrating like a birthday party in a blender. Groaning and cracking, trees shuddered and bent over double, uprooting and falling as easily as sticks in wet sand. Rain pelted us like gravel thrown by a playground bully as windows shattered and shingles ripped off the roof. As the storm surged and the ocean waves tossed and churned, spilling raging water and debris farther and farther up the beach, Momma and Poppa grabbed hold of Fish and held on tight, while the rest of us ran for cover. Momma and Poppa knew what was happening. They had been expecting something like this and knew that they had to keep my brother calm and help him ride out his storm.

That hurricane had been the shortest on record, but to keep the coastal towns safe from our Fish, our family had packed up and moved deep inland, plunging into the very heart of the land and stopping as close to the center of the country as we could get. There, without big water to fuel big storms, Fish could make it blow and rain without so much heartache and ruin.

Settling directly between Nebraska and Kansas in a little place all our own, just off Highway 81, we were well beyond hollering distance from the nearest neighbor, which was the best place to be for a family like ours. The closest town was merely a far-off blur across the highway, and was not even big enough to have its own school or store, or gas station or mayor.

Monday through Wednesday, we called our thin stretch of land Kansaska. Thursday through Saturday, we called it Nebransas. On Sundays, since that was the Lord's Day, we called it nothing at all, out of respect for

His creating our world without the lines already drawn on its face like all my grandpa's wrinkles.

If it weren't for old Grandpa Bomba, Kansaska-Nebransas wouldn't even have existed for us to live there. When Grandpa wasn't a grandpa and was just instead a small-fry, hobbledehoy boy blowing out thirteen dripping candles on a lopsided cake, his savvy hit him hard and sudden—just like it did to Fish that day of the backyard birthday party and the hurricane—and the entire state of Idaho got made. At least, that's the way Grandpa Bomba always told the story.

"Before I turned thirteen," he'd say, "Montana bumped dead straight into Washington, and Wyoming and Oregon shared a cozy border." The tale of Grandpa's thirteenth birthday had grown over the years just like the land he could move and stretch, and Momma just shook her head and smiled every time he'd start talking tall. But in truth, that young boy who grew up and grew old like wine and dirt, had been making new places whenever and wherever he pleased. That was Grandpa's savvy.

My savvy hadn't come along yet. But I was only two days away from my very own thirteen dripping candles—though *my* momma's cakes never lopped to the side or to the middle. Momma's cakes were perfect, just like Momma, because that was her savvy. Momma was perfect. Anything she made was perfect. Everything she did was perfect. Even when she messed up, Momma messed up perfectly.

I often reckoned what it would be like for me. I pictured myself blowing out the candles on my cake and fires dying in chimneys across four counties. Or I imagined making my secret birthday wish—getting my cheeks full and round with air—then floating up toward the ceiling like my very own happy birthday balloon.

"My savvy is going to be a good one," I told my brother Rocket. "I just know it."

"Girls don't get the powerful jujubes," said Rocket, running one hand through his dark shock of unkempt hair with a crackle of static. "Girls only get quiet, polite savvies—sugar and spice and everything humdrum savvies. It's boys who get the earthshaking kinds of savvy."

I had scowled at my brother and stuck out my tongue. Rocket and I both knew that there were plenty of girls climbing round our family tree that had strong and sturdy savvies, like Great-aunt Jules, who could step back twenty minutes in time every time she sneezed; or our second cousin Olive, who could melt ice with a single red-hot stare.

Rocket was seventeen and full of junk that I wasn't allowed to say until I got much, much older. But he was electric through and through, and that had always gone to his head. For fun, Rocket would make my hair stand on end like he'd rubbed it with a balloon, or hit Fish with a wicked zap from the other side of the room. But Rocket could keep the lights on when the power went out, and our family sure liked that, especially the littler Beaumonts.

Rocket was the oldest, with Fish and me following after. Born only a year apart, Fish and I were nearly the same height and looked a lot alike, both with hair like sand and straw—hair like Momma's. But while I had Poppa's hazel eyes, Fish had Momma's ocean blue ones. It was as if we'd each taken a little bit of Momma, or a little bit of Poppa, and made the rest our own.

I wasn't the youngest or the smallest in the family; broody Samson was a dark and shadowy seven, and doll-faced Gypsy was three. It was Gypsy who started calling me Mibs, when my full name, Mississippi, became far too much for her toothsome toddler tongue to manage. But that had been a relief. That name had always followed me around like one of Fish's heavy storm clouds.

The itch and scritch of birthday buzz was about all I was feeling on the Thursday before the Friday before the Saturday I turned thirteen. Sitting at the dinner table, next to Poppa's empty chair and ready plate, I barely ate a bite. Across from me, Gypsy prattled endlessly, counting the make-believe creatures she imagined seeing in the room, and begging me to help her name them.

I pushed the food around my plate, ignoring my sister and daydreaming about what it would be like when I got my very own savvy, when the telephone rang right in the middle of pot roast, mashed potatoes, and mighty unpopular green beans. As Momma rose to answer, us kids, and Grandpa Bomba too, seized the chance to plop our mashers on top of our beans while Momma's back was turned. Samson tucked some of those beans into his pockets to give to his dead pet turtle, even though Momma always said he shouldn't be giving it any of our good food, seeing how it was dead and all, and the food would just go to rot. But Samson was sure as sadly sure that his turtle was only hibernating, and Momma hadn't the heart to toss it from the house.

We were all smiling to each other around the kitchen table at the smart way we'd taken care of those beans when Momma dropped the phone with a rattling clatter and a single sob—perfectly devastated. She sank to the floor, looking for all the world as if she were staring right through the checkered brown and blue linoleum to behold the burning hot-lava core at the very center of the Earth.

"It's Poppa," Momma said in a choked voice, as her perfect features stretched and pinched.

A gust of wind burst from Fish's side of the table, blowing everyone's hair and sending our paper napkins flying pell-mell onto the floor. The air in the room grew warm and humid as though the house itself had broken out into a ripe, nervous sweat, and the many dusty, tightly lidded, empty-looking jars that lined the tops of all the cupboards rattled and clinked like a hundred toasting glasses. Outside it was already raining Fish rain—drops hastened from a sprinkle to a downpour in seconds as Fish stared, wide-eyed and gaping like his namesake, holding back his fear but unable to scumble his savvy.

"Momma?" Rocket ventured. The air around him crackled with static, and his T-shirt clung to him like socks to towels straight from the dryer. The lights in the house pulsed, and blue sparks popped and snapped at the tips of his nervous, twitching fingers.

Momma looked at Poppa's empty chair and waiting plate, then she turned to us, chin trembling, and told us about the accident on the highway. She told us how Poppa's car had gotten crushed up bad, like a pop can under a cowboy boot, and how he'd gone and forgotten to get out before it happened, landing himself in a room and a bed at Salina Hope Hospital, where now he lay broken and asleep, not able to wake up.

"Don't fret, child," Grandpa consoled Momma as though they were back in time and Momma was still a young girl sitting on his knee crying over a broken doll. "Those doctors know what's what. They'll fix your fellow up in no time. They'll get his buttons sewn back on." Grandpa Bomba's tone was soft and reassuring. But as the strobe-like flashes from Rocket's nervous sparks lit Grandpa's face, I could see the worry etched deep into all his wrinkles.

For half of a half of a half of a second I hated Poppa. I hated him for working so far away from home and for having to take the highway every day. I hated him for getting in that accident and for ruining our pot roast. Mostly, I realized that my perfect cake with its pink and yellow frosting was probably not going to get made, and I hated Poppa for wrecking my most important birthday before it had even arrived. Then I felt the burning shame of even having those thoughts about my good, sweet poppa and sank low in my chair. To make amends for my selfish feelings, I sat quietly and ate every last unwelcome green bean from beneath my mashed potatoes, as Fish's rain lashed against the windows and Rocket caused every lightbulb in the house to explode with a live-wire zing and a popping shatter, sending shards of glass tinkling to the floor and pitching the house into darkness.

Chapter 2

LATER THAT NIGHT, AS I LAY awake in the dark bedroom I shared with Gypsy, I listened to my sister's even breathing and to the steady patter of Fish's worried rain. I could hear Momma and Rocket moving around downstairs, sweeping up glass and replacing lightbulbs. And though Grandpa had gone to bed as well, every now and then the ground would rumble and the floor would shake as though the earth below us had a bellyache.

Momma and Rocket were leaving for Salina early in the morning and planning to stay in a motel near the hospital. I had begged to go, begged to go see Poppa and stay in a motel and get some of those little soaps all wrapped up in paper. But the rest of us had to stay at home with Grandpa. Rocket got to go because his electric touch was the only thing that could make the old station wagon run.

Nobody had said anything about my birthday. Nobody had said much about much. I lay awake most of the night, unable to sleep, until Momma tiptoed in with the dawn to whisper a soft good-bye, kissing my cheek lightly with her perfect pink lips. Still upset that I wasn't allowed to go with her and Rocket to Salina, I pretended to be asleep, and soon after, I heard the car doors slam and the engine rumble to life at Rocket's spark as he and Momma drove away.

That Friday before my birthday, Fish was in charge of looking after Gypsy and Grandpa Bomba. It was my job to get Samson up and ready for school and to make sure we both made it up the three steep steps of the big orange bus that took Samson and me the fifteen miles to school in Hebron, Nebraska. I had to poke and prod broody Samson up the long, soggy boggy road toward our mailbox, which had fallen over in the night after getting pushed ten feet farther to the west from all of Grandpa's worried rumbling. Samson didn't say much waiting for the bus, but Samson never did.

"It's Missy-pissy and her storm cloud," Ashley Bing said every day when Samson and I climbed onto the bus. And every day Emma Flint repeated, "Missy-pissy!" with a snorting laugh, like it was a new and funny joke each time. The kids at school had learned on my very first day that my real name was Mississippi, which had been unfortunate; we Beaumonts got enough whispers and giggles as it was. The rumors were fierce, and I'd heard them all:

"Look, it's the weird kids. My mom said they had to move here because one of them got into some *huge* kind of trouble."

"I heard the oldest brother got hit by lightning and now he's dangerous and hardly ever leaves the house."

"That family ought to live in an ark. It's almost

always storming at their place and one of these days they'll just wash away for good."

I knew that after I blew out my own thirteen dripping candles, it'd be a-di-os and a-lo-ha to Hebron Middle School, as well as to Ashley Bing and Emma Flint, and everyone else like them. After my birthday, my poor moody Samson would be a lonesome shadow in the back of the big orange bus while I grew moss in pickle jars with Fish and Rocket back at home.

It was hard for us Beaumont kids to make friends and keep them. It wasn't safe to invite anyone over with Fish and Rocket still learning to scumble their savvies; we couldn't risk someone finding out, or getting hurt by sparks or storms if my brothers lost control. Like so many things, a savvy could take years to tame, and Momma and Poppa said the ups and downs of growing up only added to the challenge.

My last day at Hebron Middle School was a slow, creeping crawl of a day. It was hard, hard, hard to concentrate on *x+y=z* when my thoughts were all tied up at Salina Hope Hospital. It was harder still to spell *accommodate* and *adolescence* and *armadillo* when I thought of Poppa waiting for Momma to come and give him a fairy-tale kiss that would wake him up, and I couldn't imagine how often in my life it might be so very important to spell *arma-double L-dillo*. But, of all things, it was hardest to listen to Ashley Bing and Emma Flint whisper and stare when the teacher said, "I'd like everyone to join me in wishing Mibs Beaumont a fond farewell. Today is her last day with us here at Hebron Middle School. Mibs will be homeschooled beginning next week."

Everyone turned in their seats to look at me. Nobody smiled or wished me a fond sort of anything. Most of the kids just shrugged and turned right back around.

"Missy-pissy's going to stay home with her mommy," Ashley said, as though she were talking to a baby—just quiet enough that the teacher couldn't hear.

"With her *mommy,*" Emma repeated.

"She's going to stay home so that no one can see what a friendless freak she is," Ashley sneered.

"What a *freak* she is," mimicked Emma like a spiteful parrot.

It was a good thing for Ashley and Emma that Momma kept us kids home once we had our savvy. By the end of the day, I was hoping that mine might give me the muscle to turn nasty girls into slimy green frogs or to glue their mouths shut tight with a nod of my head.

When Samson and I got back home that afternoon, a shiny gold minivan was parked in front of our house and Fish was angrily blasting it clean with the garden hose. With its smiling angel air freshener dangling in the front window, I recognized the van immediately. It belonged to Miss Rosemary, the preacher's wife.

Momma made the whole family go to church in Hebron every Sunday despite any fears of savvy catastrophes, and Miss Rosemary was well-known to us all. She smelled like Lysol and butterscotch and had her own matching set of rights and wrongs—like suitcases she made other people carry—and she took it upon herself to make everything and everyone as shipshape and apple-pie as she felt the Lord had intended them to be. Somehow, the news had already reached the preacher's wife about Poppa's accident and about the rest of us being on our own without a momma. Miss Rosemary had come to set things right.

Water spun from the hose in Fish's hand, swirling around the van like a cyclone in the winds churned up by his bad mood. The trees next to the house, bright yellow-green with leafy spring, bent and swayed. Fish lowered the hose when he saw us coming, his face stormy black.

"If y'know what's good for you, you'll sneak in the back." He nodded his head toward the house. We all stood and looked sadly at our own lovely house as though we'd just found out that a grizzly bear had moved in and pulled all the stuffing from the furniture and torn all the pictures from the walls and eaten all the special-occasion mini-marshmallows from the high top shelf above the refrigerator while we were gone. Then, like a break in bad weather, Fish smiled his cockeyed smile and sprayed the hose my way teasingly. "Last day away to school, eh, Mibs?"

"Last day," I said, dodging the water from the hose. Leaving Fish to finish his chore, Samson and I quietly let ourselves in through the back door—hoping to make it up the stairs before Miss Rosemary knew we were there.

"Your grandfather looked tired, so I had him lie down in his room for a rest," Miss Rosemary said the moment we entered the kitchen. She was perched up high, with a spray bottle cocked in one rubber-gloved hand and a rag held ready in the other. She was taking the jars from the tops of the cupboards and cleaning their dust with a wrinkle in her nose, squinting at the faded labels. I held my breath as I watched her, hoping that she hadn't opened any of them. No one who wasn't family should have been touching those jars—no one. "Gypsy is also down for a nap," Miss Rosemary continued. "So I expect you two to be quiet and not wake her."

"Yes, Miss Rosemary," Samson and I both said, but Samson mostly moved his lips.

"Your mother should have called me the moment she found out about your poor father," Miss Rosemary said, dusting the last jar with a flourish. Satisfied with her work, she clasped both the spray bottle and the rag to her chest and closed her eyes as though she was praying for the strength to clean up the whole wide world. When she reopened her eyes, she gave us a stern and solemn look.

"I ought to have been here sooner," she sighed. "Children need a mother in the house."

I KNEW THAT MISS ROSEMARY WAS NOT a proper replacement for our perfect momma. I knew it down in the pit of my stomach and I knew it down to the tips of my toes. A sick feeling washed over me as Miss Rosemary pointed her spray bottle dismissively toward the hallway opposite the stairs and said, "I brought Roberta and Will Junior with me to keep you company this afternoon. Why don't you two go find them? You can watch TV. *Quietly.*"

"Yes ma'am," I mumbled, even though we didn't have any TV—with Rocket in the house, Momma and

Poppa wouldn't buy any fancy gadgets until they knew, sure as sure, that my brother could keep from destroying them all accidentally.

Samson and I were eager to leave the kitchen, but not so eager to find Roberta and Will Junior, Miss Rosemary's younger children. The pastor and his wife had three children, but their older son was already thirty and worked as a state trooper in Topeka. No one talked about him much.

Roberta—who everyone but her mother called Bobbi—was sixteen, and probably only came over that afternoon because she'd hoped to find Rocket at home. Rocket, I supposed, was the kind of seventeen-year-old boy that sixteen-year-old fizgiggly girls liked to act silly and stupid around, even if he did always look as though he'd stuck his finger in a light socket.

"This is so lame," Bobbi was saying as we entered the room. "I can't believe we had to come here." Bobbi and Will Junior had never been over to our house before and were making themselves busy poking and peeking and prying. Bobbi was shuffling through a stack of Momma's half-finished paintings and Will Junior, holding one of Gypsy's wooden blocks, was prodding Samson's dead pet turtle where it lay inside a glass aquarium, pulled tight and unmoving into its shell.

"Shut up, Bobbi," said Will. "Their dad's in the hospital. Show a little sympathy."

"We don't need your sorries," I said flatly, startling Will and Bobbi, neither of whom had seen us come in. "We're doing just fine," I added.

Bobbi turned to look at me and Samson as though we were the trespassers in the room. With a heavy, well-practiced teenage sigh, Bobbi rolled her eyes, popped a big pink gum bubble, and threw herself down on the sofa with a disgusted grunt.

"Isn't there *anything* to do in this house?" she grumped, reclining and closing her eyes, laying one hand across her forehead dramatically. I noticed that Bobbi had glitter eye shadow and that her right eyebrow was pierced. A little gold hoop glinted, almost unseen, from underneath her long bangs, and I wondered how Miss Rosemary had ever allowed *that* to happen.

"Just ignore her," said Will, glaring at Bobbi, then looking kindly toward Samson and me. Will Junior was fourteen like Fish, though Will was taller and, unlike my brother, kept his curly brown hair neat. I'd always been curious about Will. I'd heard him say once that he wanted to grow up to be just like his daddy. And despite the way others at church shied away from us Beaumonts, Will always seemed to be walking on our heels or watching us when he was supposed to be praying. One time he even gave me his own cup of juice when the crowd around the punch table was too tight for me to squeeze past. But even though Will Junior and Fish were the same age and Fish didn't have a friend to his name, my brother never did like Will, thinking him to be nothing more than a holier-than-thou preacher boy. For my part, I thought he seemed nice, even if he was laced up a bit tight.

Will turned back to the aquarium. "So, is this turtle

alive or—?" He caught himself before saying "dead," grimacing apologetically.

Samson let go of my hand and coasted like a shadow across the room to pull his turtle out of its aquarium and away from Will Junior's curious inspection. After a long, unblinking stare at the older boy, Samson slipped from the room with his lifeless pet to go hide somewhere like a dusty gray moth. I knew my brother would turn up later behind a door or under his bed or beneath a pile of laundry.

Setting down the wooden block and wiping his hands on his trousers, Will Junior turned to look at me, doing a good job at mimicking a preacher's most pastorly concern.

"I hope Mr. Beaumont gets better," he said, as grave as a tombstone. "We're all praying for your dad."

"Okay." I shrugged, uncomfortable. It's not that I was against praying—I prayed every night for my savvy to come and be the best savvy ever. I prayed for the power to fly or to shoot lasers from my eyes. I also prayed for

Grandpa Bomba and for Gypsy when she caught the croup. It's just that it hadn't yet crossed my mind to pray for Poppa, and again I felt selfish and shamed and bad enough to have a house come land PLOP down on me, leaving nothing but my feet sticking out; that's just how wicked I felt.

Crossing the room, Will Junior placed one hand on my shoulder in a weird, grown-up kind of way, leaning forward with a tilt to his head like he was checking my eyes for tears.

"Mother brought you a meat loaf," he said, as if that fixed everything. I took a step back, none too sure how I felt about having Will that close—even if he was just being nice. And while I was sure meat loaf could be a powerful thing, especially if it had a lot of ketchup and the onions were chopped up real fine, I knew that tonight, for the Beaumont family, meat loaf couldn't do squat.

"A LITTLE BIRD TOLD ME THAT TOMORROW is *someone's* birthday," Miss Rosemary said with a quick, corner-of-the-eye glance from Gypsy to me as she cut a slab of meat loaf and placed it onto Grandpa Bomba's plate. The preacher's wife smiled down at the meat loaf, with its big, unfortunate, wormy onions and thin, dry layer of ketchup. I watched the knife as she cut another slice, and pretended that I hadn't heard her say anything.

Sitting at that table just then was like sitting in a pressure cooker—thanks to Fish; the air in the room went hot and taut. Only Gypsy reacted to Miss Rosemary, because she was three years old and didn't know yet what the rest of us Beaumonts knew about secrets—needing them, having them, or keeping them. Gypsy clapped her toddler hands together, eyes bright and eager in anticipation of balloons and sugar frosting.

"I thought," Miss Rosemary continued, apparently unaware of the tension—and the breeze. "I *thought* that a birthday party might help cheer everyone up a bit." She looked around the table from one face to the next. Fish stared at the salt and pepper shakers in front of him, the good crystal ones that Momma never used but kept up high in the don't-touch-or-else cupboard. I could see him trying to get a good tight grip on his savvy. It was straining him, though, and he was starting to sweat, looking pained and gray and miserable.

"*I* don't have to be there, do I, Mother?" Bobbi said, jamming a forkful of meat loaf into her mouth and rolling her eyes like she was possessed or was having some kind of fit. Part of me hoped her eyes would get stuck that way, just as people always say could happen.

"Yes, Roberta, we'll *all* be there."

"Yes, Roberta, we'll all be there," Bobbi mimicked around her mouthful of meat loaf in a frighteningly perfect imitation of her mother's voice.

"That's enough, Roberta!" Miss Rosemary shot Bobbi a look of sheer ice that thawed into an apologetic smile as she looked back at me. Bobbi slouched down in her chair.

"We'll have the party at the church, of course," the preacher's wife continued as though she'd not been interrupted. "It's rather short notice, but we can still invite all your church friends, Mibs, as well as anyone from school you'd like to ask."

"I don't have any friends, Miss Rosemary," I said, hoping that the truth might end the conversation.

"*I'm* your friend, Mibs," Will Junior said with earnest. I looked across the table at him and his buttoned-up shirt. Will grinned at me then; smiling, he looked different somehow, more relaxed. None too sure about how I was feeling toward Will Junior just then, I didn't smile back. But I didn't scowl either.

"Nonsense," Miss Rosemary continued as though Will had said nothing. "I'll show you. I'll get on the phone this evening and cook you up a fine party for tomorrow. Don't you worry, Mibs, I have *connections*." Miss Rosemary pointed one finger up to the ceiling, though I guessed she was really pointing up toward heaven. Apparently, she was going to get God to help her plan my party. I figured God had much, much better things to do, like keeping people from starving to death or from killing each other, or helping my poppa, and so I hoped He'd just stay out of it.

And I knew I wasn't the only one—I could feel Fish and Grandpa getting more and more nervous at all the talk of parties. Thirteenth birthdays in the Beaumont family were strictly non-public affairs.

I had only been eight years old back when Rocket turned thirteen, but I still remembered it as fresh and brisk as the crisp sea air. On that years-ago day at our home down south, when Grandma Dollop was still alive and Gypsy wasn't yet, Rocket and Fish and I had spent the entire afternoon in the backyard helping Grandma with her canning while Momma got the house ready for Rocket's birthday dinner.

The top of the picnic table was covered in Grandma's clear glass jars, each one with its own white label and metal lid. She'd given us kids the job of labeling the jars as she filled them. But it wasn't peaches, tomatoes, or pickles that our grandma canned, it was radio waves. Grandma only ever picked the best ones—her favorite songs or stories or speeches, all broadcast by the local stations—but still, our basement was crowded with high shelves of dusty jars filled with years and years of radio programs. How Grandma Dollop put the radio waves into those jars and got them to stay there was a mystery to me; she just had a way of reaching out and plucking them from the air like she was catching fireflies. Then she'd stuff the invisible things into the jars and tell us what to write on the labels. After that, all anyone had to do was crack the lid on any jar in her collection to hear what was inside. But you had to be careful not to take the lids off all the way, or the sounds and songs slipped out and away, lost for good unless Grandma was there and could catch them again in time.

Sitting in the backyard that day, watching Grandma capture her radio waves, Rocket had been crankier than a bear in winter. The sun had almost set on his thirteenth birthday and, so far, nothing had happened; my brother was worried that nothing ever would. Since Rocket was Momma and Poppa's first child, and Poppa came from an ordinary, everyday family with no special talents except that of losing all their hair before turning thirty, Rocket feared that he'd take after Poppa—and wind up with no savvy and no hair on his head either.

Evening fell and the sun crept down. We had just begun to carry all the jars into the house when Rocket stopped short, standing still as still with his arms full of that day's canned radio broadcasts. His skin looked pale in the early-evening glow, and he hunched over his armful of glass jars, staggering like someone had just thrown them all at him.

Grandma Dollop had stopped too, her head tilted like she was listening. I felt my hair stand up on end as an electric current ran through the air with a tingling itch.

"That's funny," said Grandma, still listening. "Something must have gone wrong at the radio station. I don't hear anything but static."

"You okay, Rocket?" I'd asked my brother carefully, worried by the pinched look on his face and the way every muscle in his body seemed to tense and tighten.

"I think I'm going to be sick," said Rocket. Then, in a blinding explosion of brilliant blue sparks, like the Fourth of July without the red or the white, my brother fell to his knees. As the jars he'd been carrying crashed to the ground and shattered, they let loose the noise of nine different radio shows at once, and a chorus of voices and sounds fluttered into the night air. At the same moment, every light inside and outside of the house went out.

Streetlamps fizzled and burst in small showers of glass and the neighbors' homes went dark all the way down the block. A blackout rolled out from our house and didn't stop until it hit the next town over.

Rocket had got his savvy and it was a shocker.

Climbing into bed on the night before my very own most important birthday, after an evening of Miss Rosemary's meat loaf and interference, I did not pray for a powerful savvy like Rocket's. I did not pray for X-ray vision or for the ability to run super-fast or to breathe underwater. I didn't pray for Grandpa or for Gypsy. I didn't even pray for Poppa to wake up.

That night, I prayed that no one—no one—would come to my birthday party.

I WOKE UP EARLY ON THAT SATURDAY morning of my thirteenth birthday and lay still and silent for a long, long while, just waiting. Nothing felt too different yet. I couldn't see through the ceiling or turn on my lamp with a blink or a wink. I couldn't float up off my mattress or make my pillows disappear.

I sighed and drum, drum, drummed my fingers against the pattern of my sheets. Nothing was happening. At least, not yet.

I decided it was safe to get up. Maybe my savvy would arrive at the church with my birthday party, bad timing and all. I rolled out of bed, glancing at Gypsy where she lay in a nest of stuffed animals and pillows. Gypsy always surrounded herself with fluff and fuzz. She liked her toddler world to be soft and smooth, with no hard edges or rough seams. Once asleep, Gypsy was as difficult to wake as a slumbering sloth.

There wasn't a creak from the floorboards or a groan from the bedsprings, but the moment my bare feet touched the floor and I stood to untwist my nightgown, my sister sat up and rubbed her eyes, staring at me from her own small bed.

"Go back to sleep, Gypsy," I said.

"No-no-no," said Gypsy, repeating her most favorite word and rubbing her eyes stubbornly.

"It's too early to be awake. Close your eyes—it's off to dreamland for you again." I crossed the room to nestle her back under her blankets, then left our bedroom quickly before Gypsy could make a fuss.

Pink light filtered through the curtains of the house, filling the hallway between the bedrooms with the faint blush of morning. I was careful not to make too much noise as I stole past the other rooms and slipped downstairs, not wanting to wake anybody else up just yet, wanting more time to myself to see what I could see, feel what I could feel.

In the kitchen, I fixed myself a bowl of cereal and took it with me into the next room to sit cross-legged on the sofa while I ate. No sooner had I gotten myself settled, balancing my bowl on my knee just right, than I heard a thump. Thump, thump, thump. I sat perfectly still, straining my eyes out across the dim room, the morning light shifting orange from pink, casting a pastel glow across Momma's stacks of paintings and glinting off the glass aquarium of Samson's dead pet turtle.

Thump.

Thump.

I set my bowl down on the floor with a splish-splash of milk sloshing up over the side and followed the thumping sound until my nose was nearly pressed up against the aquarium. There in that tank, Samson's turtle was not dead so much as living, trying its unsuccessful best to find a way up the side of the glass.

So, that turtle *had* been hibernating after all, I thought to myself. I knew that Samson would be happy— as happy as his moody broody self ever got, that is. But why had that turtle picked that peculiar, persnickety moment to wake up—there before dawn on the morning of my most important birthday, with me in my nightgown, balancing frosted cereal on my knee? Watching the turtle, I tapped on the glass. Thinking about the turtle and remembering the unusual way Gypsy had woken up as I'd stepped out of bed, a shaky and suspicious feeling started to gnaw down deep in my bones, a feeling that stuck with me the rest of the morning and continued to grow like smoke from a grassfire.

At two o'clock, we all piled into Miss Rosemary's van to head to the church in Hebron. Fish and I helped Grandpa into the front seat, reaching in to help him with the seat belt and to make sure the car radio was turned off. Ever since Grandma Dollop died, listening to the radio always made Grandpa sad.

With Grandpa settled in, Fish went back inside just long enough to find Samson and separate him from his now active, not-dead pet. Me and Miss Rosemary got Gypsy's car seat wrestled into the back as the boys climbed in. I was wearing my new special-occasion dress, the one Poppa had picked out for me all by himself at a big department store in Salina.

"I thought my little girl deserved something pretty and new to wear for her special birthday," he had said the night he handed me a big white box held closed by a thin, round strand of stretchy gold elastic. The dress inside the box was pale yellow with a high sashed waist and a full skirt that was sewn with deep pockets. Double rows of white rickrack zigzagged its way around the hem and around the seams in the short cap sleeves. But the very best part of the whole dress was the big purple flower made from soft silk ribbons that was pinned up high on the shoulder like a corsage.

"I don't know much about dresses," he'd admitted. "But I wasn't about to give up on that account. I didn't leave that store until I was sure I'd found just the right one." I pictured my poppa wandering through the store, looking for my perfect dress, and smiled.

Even with no savvy and no hair on his head, our poppa was special: He was good and sweet and had wild black eyebrows that twisted like dancing beetle legs, and a faded tattoo from his navy days—a long-haired mermaid twisting around an anchor on his forearm, just above his heavy silver wristwatch. Poppa kept Miss Mermaid hidden under crisp white shirtsleeves when he went to work in that cement and plaster office in Salina during the week. But when he came home to us at night, Poppa had his sleeves rolled up and Miss Mermaid had her smile on. And we didn't care that Poppa had no savvy, and he didn't care that the rest of us did . . . or would.

The night he gave me the dress was the last time Poppa had come home to us from Salina, the last time we'd all been together.

"Do you like it then?" Poppa had asked, rubbing his knuckles against his jaw as he watched me pull the dress from the box.

"I love it, Poppa!" I'd said, dancing my dress across the living room twice before throwing my arms around him. "Thank you!"

I knew I had the best poppa in the world, and I knew my dress was a party dress to anyone who knew anything—even if my actual party wasn't turning out the way I'd planned. Climbing up into the van, I could see Miss Rosemary eyeing the big purple flower pinned on my shoulder. I guessed she was wishing that she had a dress just like mine, instead of her straight and shapeless wear.

All buckled into the van, we bumped and jolted up the rutted road toward the highway, on our way to the church for my uninvited party. I pretended not to notice the way Fish and Grandpa kept looking at me like I was some kind of dynamite, ready to blow at the next jerk or jog of the van. I still hadn't felt any spectacular, gut-wrenching thing grip me good and firm the way it had for my brothers; I knew that my savvy was turning out to be something a bit quieter, a bit less earthshaking—yet something that would be far better for helping Poppa.

When Momma had called that morning to wish me a happy birthday, I'd asked her, "Did you kiss him, Momma?"

"Yes, Mibs. I kissed Poppa," she answered softly.

"Did he wake up?"

Momma exhaled a long, slow breath, like she was singing the last note of a lullaby, and my heart almost broke with the total sadness of it. "No, honey," she said at last, "Poppa didn't wake up. Not yet at least. The doctors say—well, they say we'll have to wait and see." At that moment, I knew exactly what I had to do—I just hadn't yet figured out *how* I was going to do it.

When we reached the church, it didn't take me long to realize that God listened better to Miss Rosemary than He did to me. The parking lot was full and there were kids everywhere. This wasn't just a little party. This was a full-on foofaraw.

If I didn't know better, I'd say Samson disappeared before the van even reached full stop, for as soon as we got out, he was gone. He'd turn up later, I knew, after spending the afternoon in some dusty hidey-hole, under the organ or with the mops in the storage closet. Grandpa Bomba just chewed his cheek and shook his head, mumbling to himself as Miss Rosemary led him and Gypsy toward the church, passing a school bus painted as pink as the bottoms of Gypsy's feet and advertising the Heartland Bible Supply Company.

Fish grabbed me by the arm as soon as Miss Rosemary had her back turned and steered me away from the pink bus and away from the church.

"You can't do this thing here, Mibs," Fish said with a gust of wind that whipped at me like a scolding. "This is no place for you to be today. Y'know it's not safe."

"It'll be all right," I assured him. "I already know what

my savvy is, Fish, and it's not going to hurt anyone. In fact—"

"You *know*?" Fish cut me off before I could tell him more. He tightened his grip on my arm. My brother's funk and squall of wind made me doubt myself for a second. But no, I was sure I was sure.

"Yes, Fish, I *know*. Just settle your storming."

Fish was looking at me expectantly. I was about to explain that I had to be the one to go wake Poppa. It was just that simple—my savvy was waking things up, just like Samson's turtle. I knew that a savvy wasn't something you could make happen for wanting, but I had proof that the means of waking up Poppa were there and wrapped up in me, ready to burst out like Rocket's sparks or Fish's wind and rain—if I could just find my way to Salina. I was about to tell my brother all of this, but at that moment Will Junior found us.

"Happy birthday, Mibs," he said, smiling. "Aren't you coming in to the party?"

"I'm coming," I said to Will, jerking my arm free from Fish's tight grip.

Fish let me go, but he gave me a look like the sharp end of a stick, and punctuated his meaning with a smattering of abrupt, uncontrolled raindrops from the clouds overhead. I gave Fish a *look* right back. Then I smiled my own smile at Will Junior and let him pull me into the church, straight into the catastrophe that was my thirteenth birthday party.

Chapter 6

STEPPING INSIDE THE OPEN DOUBLE DOORS of the church, I had the bad luck of running immediately into Ashley Bing and Emma Flint, both combed and brushed and dressed up pretty for the party. I had hoped I would never have to see either of those girls ever again after leaving Hebron Middle School for the last time. But that day, what I wanted and what I got were two very different things.

Ashley looked from me to Fish to Will Junior, resting her eyes on Will an extra-long time. Maybe it was because I was thirteen now, or because Fish and Will were there next to me, but I felt braver than I'd been at school, and I stood up tall in front of that snotty girl and her rubber-stamp sidekick.

"Why are you even here?" I said. I didn't like the way Ashley kept staring at Will, or the way her staring at him bothered me.

"My mother made me come, Missy-pissy," she said without taking her eyes off Will.

"Yeah, *Missy-pissy,*" echoed Emma.

Red-faced and mortified, I just stood there. I couldn't believe those girls had just called me that horrible name in front of Will Junior. I felt like crawling under the stained brown carpet and staying there. Fish scowled at the two girls, and a burst of wind hit us all so sharp and sudden that it sent them scurrying from the open doorway to check their hair and to fix up all their froufrou frippery. Not looking at me, Fish frowned deeper still, and I knew he hadn't meant to let loose like that in front of everyone.

"Friends of yours?" asked Will with a sympathetic smile, paying little attention to Fish, or the wind.

"Hardly," I muttered, still feeling humiliated.

He nodded. "I have a feeling you're better off without friends like that."

After that, Will Junior kindly said nothing more about Ashley and Emma. He led us past the doors of the sanctuary and past the open door to his daddy's office, where his smile faded as we paused for a moment, peeking in. I glimpsed Pastor Meeks, all tall and buttoned up, talking to some man and thumping a big pink Bible in his hands. The preacher didn't look too happy. His yellow tie hung crooked, and he was spitting as he spoke.

Running a finger inside his own starched collar, as though that top button might be making things a bit too tight, Will Junior moved us quickly past the door toward the party room. Red and orange crepe paper streamers hung sagging around the fellowship hall as though left over from another party. Aside from a large chocolate cake with no sugar roses and not a single candle, dripping or otherwise, and a small stack of hastily purchased gifts, the room was empty. Most everyone was congregating outside, probably still unsure who exactly they were there to celebrate.

Will removed a present from the stack on the table as we passed. "Happy birthday, Mibs," he repeated, handing me a small package wrapped up in colorful paper. "It's a pen set." He nodded at the gift. "In case you were wondering."

"Thanks," I said, unsure if I was supposed to open it now that I knew what was inside. But Will didn't give me the chance. Instead, he ushered us across the open room toward the kitchen, where Bobbi and two other church girls her age had been put to work making punch and peanut butter sandwiches sliced into quarters with the crusts cut off. The girls were all wearing stylish jeans and shirts that showed their skin and their belly buttons. They had pink cheeks and lip gloss and attitude to go around, and it all seemed to be spilling into the punch.

Bobbi looked at the big purple flower on the shoulder of my dress and rolled her eyes. "Happy birthday," she said in a tone that sounded more like "Drop dead." Then the other girls began to whisper and laugh as they mixed ginger ale and rainbow sherbet into pale yellow pineapple juice that was the same color as my dress.

The church girls looked past me and Fish and Will, searching the doorway as though hoping someone else might appear.

"No Rocket?" the first wondered with a sigh. Even when he wasn't there, Rocket's dark good looks and mysterious reputation won him admirers; the second girl squealed with giggles at the mention of my brother, and the first pretended to swoon. Bobbi stirred the punch with the merest hint of a smile, quickly masking it again after a teasing nudge from the other girls. Suddenly, as I looked at those teenaged girls in their teenaged clothes, I felt younger than twelve-turning-thirteen and my special-occasion dress felt not-so-special. I realized that I had just turned into a teenager myself, and there were changes coming in my life that didn't have anything to do with my savvy.

Standing in that kitchen, fiddling uncomfortably with the ribbon flower on my dress, I heard a strange and sudden sound, a sound I couldn't quite make out. But it was a sound that required my attention. Momentarily forgetting my dress and ignoring the other girls, I tilted my head, feeling ever so much like a dog listening for that whistle its owner can't hear, or like Grandma Dollop listening for just the right radio wave for her collection.

A muffled singsong voice whispered behind my ears with a sound like water still stuck there after a long swim. I shook my head and twisted my fingers in my ears. For a minute, the sound stopped. I knew that Fish was looking at me again. Watching me. He was waiting—waiting for the dynamite to blow. But that wasn't going to happen because I knew the way that things were going to be. I knew I was going down to Salina. I knew I was going to wake up Poppa the same way I'd woken up Gypsy and the same way I'd woken up Samson's turtle.

Then I heard the voice again and this time it sounded like it was right behind my eyeballs, like a headache—if a headache could be a sound. With my balance gone tipsy-topsy, I dropped my wrapped-up happy birthday pen set and bumped right into Will Junior, knocking him hard into the tray of sandwiches. The tray fell to the floor with a crash, sending triangles of bread and peanut butter flying. Bobbi cussed like a trucker with three flat tires and bent to pick up the tray. That was when I saw the picture on her skin. That was when I saw the colorful ink of Bobbi's tattoo.

The preacher's daughter had a small design on her lower back that only showed itself when she bent over in those fancy jeans. The tattoo was a picture of a little angel with a golden halo and outstretched wings, only this angel had a devilish grin and a pointed red tail to match. I couldn't fathom how Bobbi had managed to get a tattoo. I knew that if Miss Rosemary, the woman with direct connections to heaven and the ability to get God Almighty to help her plan my birthday party, if *she* ever found out, Bobbi might not make it to her *own* next birthday party, nor up to heaven to get her very own halo either.

That was when that little angel turned its head, twirled its tail, and said, *"She's really very lonely, you know . . ."*

And *that* was when I fainted.

Chapter 7

I WOKE UP TO THE SOUNDS OF quarrelsome voices. My head still felt muddled and muzzy, and there was arguing going on from every direction. I was lying on the blue plaid sofa in Pastor Meeks's office. The pastor, holding tight to a large pink Bible, was bellowing at a man so thin he'd have to stand up twice to cast a shadow.

"This—" Pastor Meeks thumped a heavy hand against the large pink Bible. "This! *This* is not what I ordered!"

"I'm nothing b-but the deliveryman, sir," the thin man stammered, his shoulders jerking. The deliveryman was wearing overalls with a button-down shirt and a stained pink necktie. There was a wilted carnation pinned to the left strap of the man's overalls and his thin hair was combed up and over his balding head like a blanket. He had a kind, sad face—like the face of a man who had just lost his dog—and he was holding a clipboard out in front of him like a shield. But neither the clipboard nor the man's sorrowful face could defend him from the preacher's hollering hoo-ha.

"When I agreed to order Bibles, no one at Heartland Bible Supply told me they were going to be pink!" spat Pastor Meeks. "What do you think we are? A church full of mollycoddled sissies?"

The deliveryman's shoulders twitched again, like he was trying to keep the straps of his overalls from falling down. But all he could manage to say was "Well, sir . . ." or "No, sir . . ." or "If you'll just sign here, sir . . ." before the preacher cut him off again.

On the other side of the room, Fish was arguing with Miss Rosemary in front of a large oak desk while Grandpa Bomba sat across from them, nodding in the pastor's big leather chair.

"Mibs doesn't need a doctor, Miss Rosemary," Fish kept saying as he grabbed for the telephone in the woman's hand. "All she needs is to go home. To go home *now*!" Fish's wind whipped through the office, blowing papers off the desk and making people's hair dance atop their heads; the deliveryman's thin hair snapped around like a bedsheet on a clothesline.

"That is for an adult to decide, young man," Miss Rosemary insisted, trying to pry Fish's fingers from the telephone. But distracted by the flying papers and the unexplained wind lashing through the room, she had no real chance at getting the phone away from Fish.

"Roger! Roger! Will you please forget those Bibles for one second and *help* me?" Miss Rosemary shouted to her husband, but the man was still too wrapped up in his upset over the boxes of sissy Bibles to pay her any attention.

"If you need an adult to decide, then let our grandpa have a say!" Fish yelled. He finally managed to get the telephone away from the preacher's wife and scrambled over the top of Pastor Meeks's desk, knocking picture frames and paperweights onto the floor as he went. Fish stood next to Grandpa Bomba, where he sat still hunched over in the leather chair. My brother raised the phone high above his head like he was daring Miss Rosemary to come and get it. "Tell her, Grandpa," said Fish.

Unfortunately, Grandpa Bomba, being as old as he was, had fallen asleep and was snoring softly. Miss Rosemary cocked her head triumphantly, resting her hands on her hips.

"Roger! I need your help!" The woman's voice was growing shrill. I could tell things were going to get far worse for us Beaumont kids than they'd been that time that Fish and Rocket had spilled red punch all over the carpet in the fellowship hall.

I sat up on the sofa, still feeling dazed.

Then, as if two squabbles weren't enough, a third ruckus overlapped the others from out of nowhere. From where I sat on the blue plaid sofa, I couldn't see where these other voices were coming from. But to my distress and dismay, the voices sounded pretty surely like they might be coming from inside my head. It felt like I had two cross and cranky gals trapped behind my eyeballs.

"This is all your fault, Carlene, you know that, don't you?" said the first whining, nasal voice.

"It's not my fault your son's dim-witted, Rhonda—you old bat," the second voice sniped back. This voice was lower, huskier, and younger-sounding than the first. I looked around the room. I couldn't see anyone else there. The voices bounced like pinballs inside my skull.

"No, you're just the one who got him delivering Bibles for your cousin Larry instead of taking that job selling coffee at the bus station. Coffee's something people will buy."

"And Bibles ain't?"

"Not pink ones!"

My head swam with the voices that seemed to belong to no one. Still sitting on the sofa, I held my head in my hands, wondering what was wrong with me. I remembered going into the church kitchen and seeing Bobbi's tattoo. Seeing Bobbi's tattoo *move*. Hearing Bobbi's tattoo speak. What had it said?

"She's really very lonely, you know . . ."

I tried to think over the noise of so many bickering voices both inside and outside of my head. I couldn't understand any of it. Nothing about what was happening felt right. What had happened to my savvy? Grandpa was asleep and I was hearing voices. With rising panic, I stared hard at Grandpa Bomba dozing in the preacher's chair. With every ounce of concentration I willed my grandpa to wake up. But the noise in the room was too much for me and I couldn't focus. I couldn't concentrate. I couldn't think. Maybe if everyone would just shut up, I might be able to make my savvy work.

I covered my ears, trying uselessly to block out all the noise. I needed to get away. I needed to get to Salina Hope Hospital. I needed to go find my poppa so that my savvy would clock in and start working right. Poppa needed me.

No one in the room had noticed that I was awake.

Pastor Meeks had his back to me. He was throwing pink Bibles into cardboard boxes and shoving them across the floor toward the deliveryman. Miss Rosemary and Fish were going round and round the preacher's desk, still fighting over the telephone. And the women's voices in my head were playing an endless tennis match of blame, blame, blame that pounded like blood in my ears.

Will Junior peeked through the crack in the door. When he saw that I was awake, he smiled, looking relieved. All I wanted to do was to get out of that room. To run away.

I waited for just the right moment for my escape, waited until I was positive no one would see me jump up quick and duck out of the pastor's office, leaving all of the arguing behind me. As I fled the room, I was thankful to find the voices of Carlene and Rhonda, the two invisible ladies, fading away. Whoever they were—*whatever* they were—they weren't following me. Outside the door, Will Junior put his hand on my shoulder again; but this time it didn't feel so strange. He'd unbuttoned the topmost button of his shirt, which made him look less grown-up and more like a fourteen-year-old boy. He was holding the wrapped-up happy birthday pen set I'd dropped when I fainted.

"You okay, Mibs?" he asked, his dark eyes filled with worry.

"I have to get out of here," I said, desperate. "You have to help me get out of here."

"I HAVE TO GET TO SALINA, WILL."

"Are you sure you're all right, Mibs?" he asked again, his hand still resting on my shoulder. "You just fainted, you know? You might be a little mixed up."

I looked Will Junior in the eye. "Please, Will. I'm not mixed up. Just help me get out of here. I need to get down to Salina."

Will Junior looked at me sadly and squeezed my shoulder. "You must miss your mom and dad a lot today, since it's your birthday and all."

I pushed his hand away and turned in the direction of the door. "I have to get to Salina," I repeated.

"Maybe Mother will drive you—" Will Junior started to offer, chasing after me.

"No, sir. I have to get there myself." I knew I was talking crazy. I had only just turned thirteen years old and already I thought I could somehow travel the ninety miles to Salina, Kansas, all by myself. But I'd hitchhike if I had to. I'd walk. There was no other way around it. I couldn't see going anywhere with a preacher's wife if I was hearing voices in my head. It was like Fish had said, the church was no place for me to be. I had to leave and I had to do it right then and there. I had to find Poppa and I had to use my savvy to wake him up. That was all there was to it.

I headed straight for the open double doors of the church. I could hear a fuss and a rumpus behind me in the fellowship hall and was certain I heard Ashley Bing's sniggering laugh, followed by Emma Flint's own copycat chortle. I watched as two boys from Samson's Sunday school class ran past me, their mouths smeared with cake. The party had started without me. I guessed it was just going to have to finish the same way.

I stepped out of the church, ready to *run* all the way to Salina if that was the only way to get there. Will Junior followed, nearly stepping on my heels.

"Hey, slow down, Mibs! Wait for me."

When we reached the parking lot, I looked around. A few kids were playing in the grass, but most everyone else was now inside the church. Fish's storm cloud hovered over the church, threatening rain.

I started walking past car after car, headed for the road. As I neared the pink Heartland Bible Supply bus, I stopped. Hearing that singsong whisper again, quiet, quiet in the backs of my ears, I saw Bobbi leaning up against the bus, all alone and chewing and snapping her gum like some kind of standoffish rebel. I supposed she *was* rather rebellious at that, what with the pierced eyebrow and the tattoo, and I guessed that that little angel with the devil's tail might've been right: At that moment, Bobbi looked lonelier than I would have ever imagined someone like her to be.

The lettering on the bus caught my eye as I tried to ignore the whispering in my head. The big letters that spelled out *Heartland Bible Supply Company* were black and peeling, past pink, down to the original school bus orange. Below that, there were smaller black letters with the address and phone number of the company. I stopped short, dumbstruck by my good fortune. The Heartland Bible Supply truck had come from no place in the world other than Salina, Kansas; it said so right there on the side in stark black paint for all the world to see. And, heeding that, I figured that if the bus had *come* from Salina, it was bound to be going *back* to Salina. Maybe God had His eye on me after all.

With a quick "thank you" to heaven, I stepped past Bobbi and her big pink gum bubble, and ran my finger along the cool pink steel of the bus, underlining the word *Salina* in the address, clearing the dust away and leaving a clean gash below the word like I had just sealed a deal.

Will Junior, still following close, raised his eyebrows high when he saw the underlined lettering on the bus. Yet he said nothing as I walked past Bobbi and climbed onto the first step just inside the open door.

Thinking about how wrong I'd been about yesterday's bus ride being my last for a while, I ignored my momma's voice in my head telling me to never ride with strangers, ignored my poppa's voice telling me to always let an adult know where I was so that I could stay safe. I tried, tried, tried to ignore the voice of Bobbi's angel talking in my head. But that proved far more difficult.

"She wonders if you're feeling all right."

"Hey, birthday-brat, what do you think you're doing?" said Bobbi, without a trace of concern bobbing up in her voice. That angel didn't really seem to know Bobbi that well.

"Get frittered, Bobbi," Will Junior said, surprising both his sister and me. "Leave us alone, or I'll tell Mother and Father about the D you got on your chemistry test." He had his hands on either side of the door to the bus and one foot resting on the first step like he planned to follow me right in.

Bobbi rolled her eyes as though she'd just been threatened by an amateur. "They'll find out about that anyway," she snorted. "And it certainly won't surprise them."

"Okay," continued Will. "Then I'll tell them about how you hoodwink the school secretary by pretending to be Mother on the phone to excuse yourself whenever you ditch."

"You think I care?" Bobbi dared him.

"She cares," said the wily voice, and I imagined that angel tattoo twirling its devil's tail. *"She'd hate to lose her secret weapon."*

"What are you two up to, anyway?" Bobbi pulled the wad of pink gum from out of her mouth and pressed it against the side of the bus, dotting the *i* in *Bible* with the sticky blob. Then she moved to take Will's place in the doorway as he and I climbed up into the bus. Through the front windshield, I saw Fish coming out of the church, dark and stormy, looking for me.

"Mibs has to get to Salina and I'm going along to see that she makes it there safe," Will Junior said to Bobbi as though God Almighty and the Great State of Nebraska had set him the task, and as though Pastor Meeks and Miss Rosemary wouldn't tan his hide for taking off without a word.

"Who do you think you are? Do you think you're Mibs's own personal safety officer?" Bobbi shouted up at her brother. "Don't you think one state trooper in the family's enough?"

For a moment, Will looked ready to explode. If the top button of his shirt hadn't already come undone, it might have popped right off from the way that Will puffed himself up.

"Shut up, Bobbi," he said. "It's only ninety miles to Salina. We'll be there in no time."

Across the parking lot, Fish had seen us and was now headed toward the pink bus, the grass next to the sidewalk waving and flattening around him as if it were under the whirling blades of a helicopter. Fish was furious.

"*You're* not going to Salina," Bobbi and I both said to Will Junior at the exact same time. Then she and I exchanged a long, squinting glare—Bobbi still standing on the ground in front of the steps, me at the top by the driver's seat, Will Junior halfway up between us, and Fish closing in fast.

Most of the tatty seats inside the bus were stacked with crates and boxes, and it looked as though several of the backseats had been removed to make room for more storage. Ignoring Bobbi and Will Junior, I headed toward the back of the bus, thinking I could hide pretty well back there until the bus got down to Kansas. Will Junior followed me in, Bobbi on his tail.

"Well, you're not going anywhere without me," she said, stomping her own way up the steps into the bus, bringing all of her sixteen-year-old spunk and hink with her. "If you two disappear, guess who'll be held responsible? Guess who'll get in trouble? Me, that's who. And if I'm going to get in trouble, it had better be for something really good. I'm going with you."

"No way, Bobbi," Will began to argue. But Bobbi held one finger up in front of her brother's face to silence him.

"*Someone's* got to look after you kids. Mom and Dad would kill me if I let you go alone."

"They'll kill you anyway," said Will. "They're going to kill us both."

"What's going on in here?" Fish demanded, as he too clambered up into the bus.

"I'm not going home, Fish," I shouted over my shoulder to my brother, climbing over boxes stacked in the aisle. "I'm going to Salina Hope. I'm going to Kansas and I'm going to find Poppa."

"On this bus?" Fish snorted.

"Yeah," said Bobbi, her sneer sounding almost cheery in its rebellion, making it seem now as though she was on my side. "We're all going to Salina, Fish-boy. If you're too scared to swim upstream with the rest of us, you may as well just hop off." Bobbi cast a sudden, swift look over Fish's shoulder and out the front window of the bus. "But make your mind up quick because I think the driver of this bus is on his way out of the church right now."

We all spun around to see that Bobbi was telling the truth. The sad-faced deliveryman was coming out of the church, carrying two heavy boxes of pink Bibles and looking downcast. Me and Will Junior and Bobbi and Fish looked at each other, waiting to see who might be first to bolt from the bus or who had the nerve to take the dare and stay on.

The deliveryman was almost to the bus when Miss Rosemary appeared in the open double doors of the church, surveying the parking lot like a prison guard.

"Quick! Hide!" shouted Bobbi. "We can't let her see us!"

In a panic, the others scrambled after me to get to the back of the old bus, tripping and slipping and bumping boxes and spilling Bibles out like pink stepping-stones across the floor. I was suddenly none too sure about this plan. Maybe I'd been too hasty. Maybe it would have been better to walk all the way down to Salina.

"She's scared," whispered the angel in my ears.

At that moment I didn't need that little tattoo telling

me how Bobbi was feeling. We were all feeling the same and nobody had time to pretend any different. Without thinking it through, I'd gotten us all hedged in on that big pink bus. We were stowaways now, unless one of us got brave enough—or crazy enough—to climb down off that bus right in front of both the deliveryman and Miss Rosemary and ruin it for everyone. But nobody made a move to flee, and I was grateful for it.

Hiding behind crates of pink Bibles, all wondering if we were awake or if we were dreaming, we dove deeper behind the stack of boxes at the back of the bus as the deliveryman climbed aboard. At the very end of the bus, we were surprised to find an army cot and a sleeping bag wedged between the boxes, along with a battered suitcase spilling out mismatched socks and extra overalls. On the floor beside those, there was a half-eaten bag of potato chips, a couple of Slim Jims, and a toppled stack of *National Geographic* magazines—some bent and faded, others crisp and new.

The biggest surprise, though, was Samson.

Samson had pulled himself into a tight ball underneath the cot, like his turtle in its shell. He'd been looking at the pictures in one of the old, old magazines, with his wide dark eyes open to an article titled "Strange Habits of Familiar Moths" when we invaded his hiding space. But Samson didn't even bother to look up until the big noisy rattle of the bus's engine set the bus to vibrating.

I held my finger to my lips, warning Samson unnecessarily to keep quiet, forgetting for a second that my broody, moody brother was *always* quiet and that it would take more than a bit of volume to be heard over the grind and growl of that old bus. As the wheels started turning, we all grabbed on to whatever we could to keep ourselves from bumping and bouncing all around as the bus rolled out of the church parking lot and out toward the highway. But then that big pink Bible bus reached Highway 81 and turned left instead of right, north instead of south—and we were suddenly headed away from Kansas, not toward it.

Chapter 9

REALIZING THAT WE WERE HEADED FARTHER and farther up into Nebraska, Fish and I scrambled to our knees to peer out the window. Fish gave me a bug-eyed, hard-faced look that said: *Now What?* with a *This-Was-a-Stupid-Idea* tang to it.

Apparently not caring which way we were headed, Bobbi settled down like Cleopatra on the cot, propped up on one elbow and pressing her weight down onto Samson, who was still curled up quiet underneath. Bobbi pulled a large roll of Bubble Tape from her pocket, tore off a good-sized strip, and jammed it into her mouth. Then she picked up one of the newer issues of

National Geographic from the top of the pile and started casually flipping through its pages. The magazine had a picture of a human heart on the cover, looking like nothing more than a big ball of watermelon threaded through with pale roots; I thought that picture made a person's heart look like a fragile, fragile thing rather than the powerful muscle that I'd learned it to be in school. I looked at Bobbi then, and realized that she might just be the same way—tough and soft at the same time. She was stretched out on that cot like she was back home on her very own sofa. If that angel hadn't been whispering in my head, telling me how Bobbi was just as nervous as the rest of us, I would've thought that she had no cares at all, that she was just a powerful sixteen-year-old muscle.

Fish perched himself, elbows on knees, as far from Bobbi on the cot as he could get, which put him down on the end by her feet. As he balanced on the edge of the canvas and metal bed, I could feel Fish's older-brother eyes burning through me. I knew he was mad. I knew he was worried. I imagined he was hearing Momma and Poppa in his head too, and was feeling like he had to be the responsible one. Mostly, I knew he was remembering his own hurricane and all the damage that got done just because he turned thirteen in the wrong place.

I sat down on the floor, still sure as sure that this bus would turn around and head back toward Salina, Kansas, in no time flat. I pulled my knees up tight to my chest and pulled my soft yellow skirt down all the way to my ankles; that big purple flower tickled my cheek like it was trying to make me smile. Will Junior sat on the floor next to me, even though it was dirtying his trousers. He sat, not quite touching my hand with his, the happy birthday pen set resting in his lap, still wrapped up in birthday paper.

As the bus rattled on and on, away from Kansas and Poppa in his hospital bed and Momma and Rocket in their motel with white soaps and towels, I could hear the hush-hush tattletale of Bobbi's angel in my head. I tried to ignore it, to pretend I didn't hear it.

I remembered seeing a crazy man once when we lived down South, a man who was weaving and wandering along a downtown sidewalk talking to no one but himself; talking and smacking himself on the side of the head like he was trying to get something to pop out the other side. Like he had a bug in his ear—or like he was hearing voices. I wondered if that was where I might be headed. It was the stress, I told myself, the stress of all my worry for Poppa, the stress of trying to figure out my new savvy and make it work right. Stress made people's minds do funny, funny things.

I tried to ignore the angel's humming, crooning voice the same way I'd ignored the hissing whispers of Ashley and Emma and all the other kids at Hebron Middle School only yesterday, and every day before that, every day since we'd come to live in Kansaska-Nebransas. But as I pushed that voice to the back of my head the way I swept crumbs under the stove when Momma wasn't looking, I realized that beneath the sound of the angel, beneath the racket of the bus and the rustle of the boxes, the squabbling ladies from Pastor Meeks's office were back in my head as well. Carlene and Rhonda were back—and they were still quarreling.

"The man doesn't use the few brains God gave him. He can't even make a proper delivery. How hard can it be to drop off a crate of Bibles?" said Carlene in her deep, graveled voice.

"It's not hard to sell coffee. He should'a just done that," the older voice of Rhonda snapped back. *"You never did know how to take care of my boy. What he saw in you, I'll never know."*

The voices sounded like they drifted back to me from the front of the bus over an intercom linked directly to my brain. I knew that no one other than the deliveryman had gotten on that bus except us kids, and I was pretty certain that no one else could hear what I was hearing.

I dropped my forehead to my knees and rocked my head from side to side, trying to concentrate on the texture of the pale yellow fabric of my special-occasion dress against my skin, trying not to listen to the bickering old bats as they continued to blame each other for the deliveryman's misfortunes.

I had no idea how much time passed as the bus thundered and rumbled up the highway. It felt like hours. I could see the sky go by outside the windows above me and watched an unending parade of telephone poles flick past like the ticks and tocks of a clock. Silos and water towers marked the distance between towns along the highway, but every time I rose up high enough to look out, all I saw was the same seemingly endless, sleeping landscape—field after field of last summer's dead brown cornstalks and rows of lifeless, skeletal irrigation equipment, all waiting for the earth to wake up with spring and ask for a drink of water.

My backside began to fall asleep and a cramp started to pinch my leg as the late-afternoon sun slanted low and long and bright through the windows of the bus, casting big rectangle shadows off the boxes of Bibles.

It was just about that same time that Bobbi got bored.

With a nasty smirk, she lifted one foot and kicked Fish off the end of the cot. Temper flaring, his face contorted, unable to control his savvy as vexed and tense as he was, my brother let loose.

Magazines flew up into the air like an angry flock of helter-skelter, yellow-winged birds, caught in the updraft of Fish's fury. Cardboard lids from boxes and crates flapped and fluttered, and the windows of the bus steamed up and shuddered with the force of Fish's frenzied squalls. Bobbi covered her head with both her arms as the magazines jetted over her, threatening to dive down as the heat inside the bus became downright tropical. I imagined Bobbi getting shredded up by paper cuts from those flailing, flying magazines, and I jumped up from the floor to grab on to Fish, who had his eyes locked on and burning at Bobbi. I took my brother by the shoulders and gave him a right hard shake. I thought for one ghastly grim moment that I might have to slap him or slug him or twist his ears—anything to get him to stop storming.

"Fish!" I hissed his name and shook him again, feeling desperate. Suddenly Samson was at my side. As calm as calm, without a smile or a frown or a blink of his eyes, Samson put one pale hand on Fish's arm. He didn't squeeze or pinch or smack or cuff. Samson just touched his dusty fingertips to our brother's wrist and the whirlwind stopped.

Fish broke his fiery gaze away from Bobbi and looked down at Samson, shaking his head a couple times, as though to clear the last gusts of rage from his brain.

"Sorry," he said, looking cross and fuddled, red-faced in his apology to Samson or to Bobbi or to himself. Will Junior had gotten up from the floor during Fish's outburst, dropping the pen set and accidentally kicking it beneath the cot as he batted at the attacking magazines. Now he and his sister were looking at my brothers and me like we were aliens just landed green and mean in their backyard. Everything had gone quiet . . . and I mean everything. It took me a moment to realize *how* quiet things had got . . . and how still.

The bus had stopped. The engine had been turned off. The rattling and bouncing had halted. The deliveryman was standing in the aisle, fists on hips, arms akimbo, staring at us all, his lost-dog look replaced now by something a bit more nettled—something a lot more cross.

"She knows she's in trouble now," said Bobbi's angel in my ears.

She's not the only one, I said to myself.

IN THE DEAFENING SILENCE, THE DELIVERYMAN looked at us as though deciding what to do about finding baby mice nesting in his Bibles—would it be poison or drowning? Would he feed us to a cat, or stick us in a trap? He looked at us and we all looked back at him, hardly daring to breathe.

The man had removed his wilted carnation and loosened his pink necktie. He had his sleeves rolled up at the cuffs, and when he folded his arms across the front of his faded overalls over his narrow sunken chest, Carlene and Rhonda, the sassing and squabbling ladies, finally showed their faces—or rather, their places.

Carlene was tattooed in fancy letters on the man's right arm above a black rose with thorns like nails. *Rhonda* was tattooed on the man's left arm beneath a red heart with the word *Mom* inscribed inside it. As I watched, the letters of each name eddied and jived; my stomach turned over as the lines began redrawing themselves into the likeness of women's faces. Their argument started up again.

"You're his mother, Rhonda. What did you do to make Lester grow up so soft? The man's got no fight."

"Don't blame me! Lester takes after his useless fool of a father, the weak man. But maybe, Carlene, if you didn't insist that my boy give you every nickel and dime he makes from delivering those Bibles for your cousin, Lester would have a chance at getting ahead for once in his life, instead of suffering to support your lifestyle."

I watched the two women, animated from the lines of their own names like comic strips in the Sunday funnies come to life, and I felt my head go filmy and fuzzy again. I took a step back, weak-kneed and shaken, trying to remind myself that *this* was not my savvy. This was just my mind playing tricky, tricky tricks on me. I still had to get to Poppa and wake him up, because *that* was what was supposed to happen. I wanted to sit down on the cot before my jelly legs gave out, but Bobbi was still stationed there and Will Junior was standing in the way.

Then Samson was in the corner of my eye like a ghost, his tender touch brushing my back. I no longer felt like I would fall, and I could blink my eyes against the yammering women and begin to scumble their voices to a slightly lower volume by relaxing and taking some deep breaths.

"What are you k-kids doing b-back there?" the deliveryman said, his voice galled and glum yet surprisingly tuneful, like a country western singer yodeling from atop a cactus. None of us said anything, not knowing what to say or who should say it.

"Now, don't make me repeat myself," the man said, still musical but jittery, as though talking to kids gave him the jimjams.

"That's right, Lester," said Rhonda from the man's left arm. *"Show them your backbone."*

"Oh, like he's got some kind of gumption," scoffed Carlene. *"He'll make a good short show of it before he crumbles. These kids'll be driving this bus and telling him where to sit in less than ten minutes."*

Swallowing hard, I took a small and careful step toward the man. "Are you headed back down to Kansas anytime soon, sir? We were just trying to get to Salina."

Lester looked down at me, arms still crossed, straining to keep his thin shoulders still as he did his best to stand his ground. His mouth worked like he was chewing on a strip of Bobbi's gum and trying to keep wrong words from forming in it. He struck me as a fellow whose gears might turn a bit slower than those of other folks, a man whose thinking cap had gotten shrunk in the wash and now fit his brain a notch too tight.

"You k-kids can't be on this b-bus," the man said finally, extending one arm with a finger pointed our way.

But the finger shook as Carlene laughed and Rhonda scolded, ridiculing Lester's attempts at grit and fortitude, and the man's eyes held no real spite or spleen.

"Please, sir." I took another step forward. "We're just trying to get to Salina. We'll keep out of trouble and out of the way. Surely it couldn't hurt for us to hitch a ride with you. You've got plenty of space. You're going back there, aren't you? The sign on your bus says—"

"I could get into a mighty b-big heap of trouble having k-kids on my bus," Lester stammered, taking one step back and tucking his pointing finger back under his dampening armpit as though he couldn't trust it. "My b-boss wouldn't like it one bit. He'd fire me, that's what he'd do. Do your folks know where you are?"

"My momma and poppa are down in Salina right now, sir. My poppa's in the hospital. You'll be doing them a great big favor bringing us down to them. I swear." I raised one hand in the air like I was taking an oath; surrounded by all of those Bibles, I thought it had to count for something. Lester rocked back and forth on his heels, shoulders still wiggling, gears still grinding.

"Here he goes. That's Lester Swan," Carlene said. *"Caving in like a dunkle-head to a little girl."*

Rhonda clucked her animated tongue in motherly disappointment. *"It never did take more than a tap to knock my Lester to the ground. If only he'd turned out more like me. I'd show these kids what for."*

Lowering my hand, I took another step forward; Lester Swan took a second step back as though he thought I might bite him if I got too close.

"Please, sir?"

Lester ran his right hand through his thin hair, scratching at the bald head underneath and making the bit of tuft he had left stick up like the feathers of an ugly duckling; Carlene rolled her cartoon eyes as she rocked up and down and upside down with the motion. For a moment I thought Lester would kick us off the bus right there and then, leaving us on the side of the highway in the middle of nowhere. But after an awkward, wordless standoff, the moment passed, and Lester sank down to sit on the edge of the nearest seat with an extra slump and sag to his shoulders.

"So, where are you all from?" he asked with the sorry voice of a man who'd just lost the last of his pluck and knew it.

IT TURNED OUT THAT LESTER SWAN enjoyed having folks to talk to. Clearing off the first rows of tatty, ratty seats, he pressed us all to sit up at the front of the bus while he drove. Bobbi and Will Junior sat on one side of the bus, just behind the driver's seat, suddenly none too sure about us Beaumont kids and the funny, funny things that happened around us. Me and Fish sat together across the aisle, both anxious to get back on our way. Samson preferred to keep to himself in the back, slipping again underneath the cot with the bag of potato chips, the Slim Jims, and the pile of magazines at his fingertips.

"This ol' gal may have some faulty p-pistons, and

her c-carburetor may need replacing, but she's still got some miles left in her," said Lester, rambling on to us about the big pink delivery bus as he drove. He talked about that bus like it was a delicate, niminy-piminy thing that depended on him for its constant care and looking after. "Of course, I do well to remember to keep her b-below fifty-four miles an hour." Lester grimaced, screwing up his face like he was remembering all the times he *hadn't* remembered. "Anything over that, and this old b-bus just quits. I remember one time when—"

"Just how long 'til we get to Salina?" Fish wanted to know, interrupting Lester's ramble impatiently. "Our poppa's in a bad way. We need to get down there soon." My heart skipped and my stomach twisted as I remembered Momma's words: *The doctors say we'll have to wait and see.* Will and Bobbi shifted nervously, as they too recalled the reason we'd all climbed aboard that bus in the first place.

"Well," said Lester, flustered by the bugaboo of having to change mental road maps mid-sentence. "Let me think. I have to get on up to Bee b-before five." Keeping one hand on the steering wheel, Lester pulled a watch with a broken strap from the pocket of his overalls.

"Doggone it!" he said, nearly driving off the road as he stared at the watch. "I'm late." The bus heaved and rattled as Lester stepped harder on the gas. Remembering everything he'd just finished telling us about the big pink bus breaking down if it went too fast, Fish and I kept a close and nervous eye over Lester's shoulder at the speedometer.

"So then," Fish continued. "After Bee? Will you be going back to Salina when you get done there?"

"Hmm?" Lester looked back at Fish distractedly, as though he hadn't been listening. "After Bee? Naw, I still have to go on over to Wymore, then I have to make a quick stop down in Manhattan to p-pay some money to a lady friend—it's her cousin Larry who's my b-boss and she gets real mad if I don't bring the money by. After *that,* we'll be headed back to Salina."

By this time, Bobbi had slid to the edge of her seat; she was peering intently around the barrier between her and the back of Lester's seat and scowling at the deliveryman. "Just how long is all that going to take? Exactly *when* are you planning on getting back?"

"Oh, no later than tomorrow afternoon, I s'pose," said Lester absently as he took an exit off the interstate and headed still farther north, farther from Salina, onto a small rural highway.

"Tomorrow?" we all shouted. *"Tomorrow?"*

"That's too long!" I cried.

"Well, there's nothing I can d-do about that," said Lester, trying hard to end the conversation. "I can't afford to lose my job. If I go b-back now, I'll be fired for sure. Then it will be no Bibles, no b-bus, and no future for poor old Lester."

I swallowed hard, caught between that rock and that hard place I'd heard mentioned so often, and understanding fully now what a bad spot that truly was. How could I ask a man I didn't even know to risk his livelihood on my account? But, how could I possibly wait another day to get to Poppa?

"Tomorrow. That's just great." Bobbi turned and looked at me, her eyes bulging in disbelieving voodoo vibes. *"Tomorrow,"* she repeated once more, nodding her head and leaning back against her seat. "That's *wonderful.*"

Fish and Will Junior were looking my way too. I cringed and sank down in my seat, feeling wretched and troubled over our new situation. To my surprise, Will winked my way with a crooked smile, making me feel a bit better. Out of everybody on that bus, Will was the only one who looked like he might be having fun.

The itty-bitty town of Bee, Nebraska, was just about the size of a yellow striped bumbler; it could buzz right by you if you blinked too slow. As though the situation wasn't bad enough for us already, things went even more catawampus and cockeyed once we got to that teeny-tiny town.

There was only one church in Bee. It was built boxy and angled like an accordion, but the windows of the church were dark, and the doors were locked up tight.

Lester Swan looked from his watch toward the sun—now barely visible on the horizon—all the while tugging the door handles and pacing the bright green Astroturf leading up to the side door. He sat down on the cement step of the church and scratched his head. I wandered away to avoid listening to Carlene and Rhonda blister and bellyache over Lester's latest blunder. Those two gals pickled me, they were so sour. Thinking about my own momma, I felt sorry for Lester. Rhonda's voice was nothing like what a momma's ought to be. Of course, my momma was extra-special, I reminded myself. My momma was perfect.

"It took months for me to figure out my savvy when I was your age," I remembered Momma telling me one day. We had been in the kitchen, me and Momma and Gypsy, and Momma had been trying to teach me how to make a perfect pie crust. But my crust was far from perfect. Gypsy had been more interested in squishing her fingers deep inside her own small lump of soft dough, pulling out pinches and eating them when Momma's head was turned.

My crust had kept on crumbling and breaking, or sticking and tearing; I'd smash it back together and try rolling it out again and again, while Momma's crust lifted up clean and easy, spreading out across the bottom of the pan as soft and smooth as silk—perfect as perfect.

"How *did* you know, Momma?" I'd asked, flour tickling my nose and falling like snow from the edge of the table where I stood with my own large rolling pin. "How did you figure out your savvy? When did you first know that you were perfect?"

Momma looked down at the mess on the table and laughed; the sound was like the church bells in Hebron on a clear morning. At first I thought Momma might be laughing at my wounded and weary blob of dough, then

I remembered that my momma would never do such a thing. She pulled one of the kitchen chairs up close and sat down, setting aside my rolling pin and taking my floured and dusty hands in her own. She smiled up at me with a sweet smile.

"I'm not perfect, Mibs. Nobody's perfect. I just have a knack for getting things right. Maybe that looks a lot like perfect sometimes. Besides," she continued, her smile faltering a bit as she squeezed my hands, "you'd be surprised at how many people dislike spending time with someone who constantly gets things right. It's not always an easy way to be."

I nodded at Momma as she hugged me. I was hardly able to imagine anyone not wanting to spend time with her.

"In most ways, Mibs, we Beaumonts are just like other people," Momma said, letting go of me and adding a bit more flour to my dough as she recited the words I'd heard so many times before. "We get born, and sometime later we die. And in between, we're happy and sad, we feel love and we feel fear, we eat and we sleep and we hurt like everyone else."

I thought about Momma as I walked around the side of the church and up the rutted dirt road a short way, listening with relief as the voices faded and an ensemble of crickets began warming up their evening act—maybe I'd woken them up, I mused to myself. Kicking at rocks, I crossed the road and headed toward an old boarded-up and falling-down house that looked as though a truckload of white paint had dropped on it from top to bottom once upon a time ago. Fish had stayed on the bus with Samson; he was still stewing and grouchy and was now almost as quiet and broody as our little brother. Bobbi was outside the bus chewing on a new length of Bubble Tape and cursing under her breath, so we all gave her plenty of distance.

I stepped up onto the porch of the old house cautiously, thinking that a porch swing would have made it a perfect place, once upon a time. Since we didn't have our own in Kansaska-Nebransas, Poppa would take us to the World's Largest Porch Swing in the park in Hebron. That swing could hold fifteen people at one time. Poppa would load the whole family into the station wagon and let Rocket's spark drive us up there on Sunday afternoons to sit all together on that long, crazy swing that had no porch attached.

"Just use your imagination, Mibs," Poppa would say when I complained that a swing couldn't be a porch swing without a porch. "Close your eyes and imagine what kind of a grand house might have a porch swing this size." I'd do as he said, but the only place I ever pictured was our own home.

"Every good country home needs a place to sit and think and watch the clouds roll by," Poppa had said to me. Poppa wanted to build us our very own swing, it was always near the top on his list of important things to do. I knew I had to get to Poppa soon. I couldn't let anything happen to him, not with that list left unfinished—he wouldn't want to abandon our dreams. He'd want to build that swing so that we could all sit there together.

The porch creaked and groaned. I turned around to find Will Junior standing on the porch behind me. He didn't come close, like he'd done before. Now he had his hands in his pockets and was looking at me as though he'd never seen a girl before.

"What's going on, Mibs?"

"What do you mean?" I said, not looking at him straight on.

"I mean, maybe you should start telling me what happened back there on the bus with Fish and that storm of wind," Will Junior said, still studying me.

I ran my hand across the porch rail, absently brushing at the peeling paint that covered the old gray wood like lacy splinters, still not able to stare Will Junior in the eye.

"I don't know what you want me to tell you," I said, feeling false and fickle, knowing exactly what he wanted to hear and knowing that I could never tell him. When I braved a glance at his face, I could see that Will's eyes were bright and eager with curiosity, like a small child waiting for a parade to come around a corner.

"I've always known there was something different about you, Mibs Beaumont, and your brothers too," Will Junior said. I shrugged my shoulders, not agreeing, but not saying anything either.

"Don't get me wrong—I like that about you," Will added awkwardly, stepping a bit closer.

Surprised and embarrassed, I stood speechless on that porch until the silence grew itchy and uncomfortable. Searching desperately for some way to change the subject, I rounded fully on Will Junior and demanded in a fluster, "So, just why are you called Will *Junior,* anyway? I know your daddy's not Will *Senior*. His name's not even *William,* for heaven's sake."

He smiled back at me with a devilish grin. "Maybe you're not the only one with a secret, Mibs."

I looked up and down at that boy, and for some reason I couldn't help but smile back at him, even if it did make my cheeks burn red.

"I suppose I can live with that," I said finally, like

he and I had come to some kind of arrangement. Our secrets would stay secrets.

Will Junior pulled one hand out of his pocket. He was holding the wrapped-up happy birthday pen set. He'd retrieved it from the floor of the bus, and now he held it out to me. The bright wrapping was ripped on one side and a bit worse for the wear.

"It's still your birthday, you know."

I took the present from Will and smiled even wider. He was right. It was still my birthday and I hadn't yet opened a single present. I stuck one finger into the tear on the side and ripped the paper away from a thin hinged box. A gust of wind I hoped did not belong to Fish swept the wrapping paper out of my hands and sent it up and across the road and away from us. Opening the box, I found two fine and fancy ballpoint pens with shiny silver finger grips and rounded caps. I set the box down on top of the porch rail and pulled out one of the pens.

"I could have tried writing something if that paper hadn't blown away," I said. Will Junior swept his arm out in front of him with a gallant gesture before kneeling down on the cracked and flaking boards at my feet, like he was a grown-up man proposing. He held one hand out to me, palm up, offering it as a writing surface.

Nervously, I took his hand in mine. The blue ink flowed out smooth and easy against Will Junior's skin, and in a moment I'd drawn a smiling sun. The next moment, I jolted backward, tripping over a jutting porch plank and falling onto my tail end, as that smiling sun blinked its eyes and cleared its throat like it had just woken up.

Like it had just woken up, and now it had something to say.

Chapter 12

BEFORE THE BLUE INKED SUN COULD utter a word, I picked myself up and ran away from Will Junior and the falling-down house. I ran past Lester Swan where he sat with his feet on the Astroturf, and past Bobbi and her gum bubble. Up the steps and into the bus, I ran straight past Fish, where he sat hunkered and grumpy in the front seat. I didn't stop until I'd pressed myself underneath the cot in the back of the bus, pushing in next to Samson, who moved over without a question or a word as though he'd been expecting me. I plugged up my ears with my fingers. I squeezed my eyes shut and began to hum, hum, hum, hum, hum.

It was no good. I could still hear them all. As Lester and Bobbi climbed back onto the bus wondering what was wrong with me, I could hear Carlene and Rhonda and the little angel with the pointed devil's tail all there inside my head. But now I could hear a new voice too, the voice of the smiling blue sun, gaining volume like a deep-toned bell as Will Junior climbed up into the bus.

"A secret for a secret for a secret . . . Will has a secret. Want to know the secret?"

Not knowing what else to do, I shouted, "You have to wash your hand, Will Junior!" though it sounded stupid, even to me, as my voice echoed through the quiet bus over the din of voices in my head. I didn't want to know Will's secret. I didn't want to know things I wasn't supposed to know.

"Mibs? Are you okay?" Will called out to me as he made his way down the aisle of the bus, the voice of that noisy blue sunshine growing louder and louder as he got closer.

"Will's got a secret . . ."

"Don't come near me!" I shouted back at him.

Fish, seeing me upset and not bothering to find out what might have happened, closed in on Will Junior and spun him around, clocking him hard and fast in the eye with his fist. Will took the blow, stumbling backward along the aisle of the bus, and Bobbi joined the scuffle, climbing over the seats and throwing herself at Fish, scratching his cheek with her fingernails.

Ignoring Bobbi and scrambling after Will Junior, Fish demanded, "What did you do to my sister? What did you do to her?"

"Will's got a secret . . . Want to know the secret?"

"WASH YOUR HAND, WILL JUNIOR!" I screamed again, raising my voice to be heard over the brawl and over the sound of breaking glass. As my brother's pressure system grew, the windows closest to Fish began to fracture, spreading splintering cracks outward like spiderwebs zipping and pinging through the glass as Fish's gusts and gales swelled in speed and strength. Bobbi screamed and Lester cried out as first one and then another window shattered outward. Ducking and dancing and wincing and flinching with every new explosion of glass, Lester grabbed both boys by their collars and pushed and pulled and dragged them off his bus with Bobbi following after.

". . . a secret for a secret for a secret . . ." Quieter now, but still that ink doodle sun yammered in my brain. I scrambled from beneath the cot and peered out of the nearest broken window.

"Please, Will, just go wash that ink off your hand!" I shouted, knowing he couldn't understand. Now outside the bus, Fish's wind blew out across the parking lot and through the trees around the church. A dark storm cloud was forming overhead and a smattering of rain began to pelt the ground. It was a good thing we weren't too close to any large bodies of water, or that storm over Bee could have been one to rival Fish's worst.

Crunching on the broken glass that lay scattered across the parking lot, Fish suddenly stopped struggling against Lester Swan and looked up at my face in the window.

He looked at me screaming and plugging my ears and at the tears dripping like the kitchen tap down my cheeks; my words finally hit him, and he listened. Fish twisted sharply from me to Will Junior as though suddenly adding two and two and getting twenty-seven, even though most people could only ever get four. Storm subsiding, he grabbed Will by the wrist to behold the drawing of the sun inked in blue on his palm. My brother took one last look up from that simple doodle to my sorry, sorry self framed inside the broken window. Then, understanding that my upset must have something to do with the unexpected things that happen when a Beaumont turns thirteen, Fish did what he had to do.

Still holding tight to Will's wrist, Fish worked his mouth for one long second, then spat a big, thick wad of juicy spit right into Will Junior's hand.

"*Eww,* man!" Will hollered out in disgust. "That's just foul!" Will tried to pull his hand away, but Fish held on tight, smearing that spit in and around to mix with the ink until there was nothing left but a great messy smudge, resembling nothing much more than the big blue-black bruise that was already forming around Will Junior's eye where Fish had popped him a shiner.

"Let go already!" Will demanded, pummeling at Fish with his free fist.

With Fish's spit, the new voice in my head gurgled and gargled and sputtered and spluttered until *"secret"* turned to *"slucbret,"* and *"slucbret"* turned to *"sluppet,"* and *"sluppet"* slipped away like water down a drain, leaving Will Junior's secret safe and only three voices remaining in my head.

Lester Swan was doing his best to keep the boys apart and Bobbi off his back, skating and sliding on the broken glass. As soon as Fish saw the muscles in my face relax and my shoulders drop back down to where they normally rested—as soon as he saw the relief in my eyes—my brother backed off, pulling free from Lester's grip and stepping out of the way of Will's fists. Fish may not have known precisely *why* he'd needed to get that ink doodle off Will Junior's hand, but he'd known it was important to *me,* and I was grateful. Sometimes it was good to have older brothers.

Looking grossed-out and suspicious, Will Junior wiped his wet and sullied hand on his trousers. His shirt had come completely untucked and his hair was wild and unruly above his blackening eye.

I realized I was still holding tight to the fine and fancy silver pen that Will had given me. It felt heavy in my hand, like it was made of lead. I replaced the cap on the writing end and slipped the pen into one of the deep pockets in my skirt; I'd left the box and the other pen back at the falling-down house. I was worn out and tired, and I didn't think I liked being a teenager all that much. As the last ray of sun surrendered to the deep blue of evening, I sank to the floor of the bus, trying again not to think, and not to listen.

"What's Lester gotten himself into this time?" muttered Carlene behind my eyeballs.

And Rhonda answered with a cluck of her tongue: *"The usual trouble, of course. The usual trouble."*

Chapter 13

AS LESTER SWAN LOADED THE OTHERS back onto the bus, assigning them seats well away from each other and surveying the damage to the windows mournfully, I tried making a deal with God. I vowed that I would eat my green beans without complaint, I'd be a good person, and I'd never take more than one half of a powdered sugar donut after Sunday school ever, ever again. If only I could stop hearing voices when someone nearby had ink on their skin—especially voices that insisted on sharing secrets and feelings others preferred to keep hid.

I hadn't cried once since Poppa's accident, but now

that I'd started, there on that big pink bus, I couldn't stop. Everything felt broken and hopeless. What if this had all been for nothing? What if Poppa was already better and sitting up in bed laughing and talking with Momma and Rocket? Or what if Poppa was worse; what if he was . . .

I sobbed harder, trying to push my worst fears out of my mind. Samson wiggled out from under the cot, dragging the almost empty bag of potato chips and the Slim Jim wrappers with him. Sitting down on the floor next to me, offering me the last salty crumbs of chips without a word, he rested one gentle hand on my arm.

I'm not sure what it was about my shy and shadowy Samson, but his touch always made a person feel more braced up inside. It happened now and then, I knew, that some folks got their savvy early. Momma's brother, Uncle Autry, had five-year-old twin girls who could make their plastic ponies hover an inch or two above the ground as they played, moving them up and down like carousel horses. But, outside of our cousins, that sort of thing was rare. Maybe it made a difference that the girls were twins and seemed to share a savvy between them.

Perhaps Samson's strengthening touch was just an ordinary sort of human magic, the kind of magic that exists in the honest, heartfelt concern of one person for another. Regardless of the reason, with Samson's small hand on my arm, it wasn't long before my eyes began to dry.

"What's the half-baked idiot thinking? Lester should have his head examined," Rhonda was saying from Lester's left arm. *"How could any son of mine turn out to be such a namby-pamby?"*

"What he should do is leave these rotten kids on the side of the road, the same way I ditched that mangy dog of his when the beast chewed up my best red shoes," said Carlene from his right. *"Instead the dolt bandages their boo-boos and pats them on the head."*

I knew I didn't care much for Lester's mom, Rhonda, and I was certain I didn't care at all for Carlene. But Lester

Swan must have felt something strong for each of them, having seen the need to tattoo their names right on his skin. To me, those two seemed like heavy ladies to heft around. Rising to my knees, I peered up over the seats and boxes through the dimming light to watch Lester root around under the driver's seat, then come up, looking triumphant, with a rusty old metal box with a red first aid cross on it. He handed the box to Bobbi, who looked at it like Lester had just handed her a dead rat.

"What do you want me to do with this?" Bobbi asked.

Lester hemmed and hawed as he pointed toward the first aid kit. "Maybe you could tend to the b-boys so that I might try to c-cover some of these windows and get us b-back on the road?"

"I don't *tend,*" said Bobbi, sounding snarly and sarcastic with her lip pulled into a sneer. "What do I *look* like? A nurse?"

"Naw, you just look like the oldest," Lester said with a crooked half smile, though his shoulders twitched again, nearly jumping all the way up to his ears this time. He crossed and uncrossed his arms as though trying to figure out how to look like he required listening to.

"This is all Mibs's fault. Make *her* tend," said Bobbi, handing the first aid kit back to Lester.

Twitch. Twitch. Lester took the box back from Bobbi and looked down the length of the bus, catching my eye where I peered over the last seat. Even through the gloom of nightfall, I could recognize the look of a drowning man when I saw one. I couldn't stand to listen to Carlene and Rhonda snicker and scoff as Lester sank below the tide of Bobbi's attitude. Maybe this was my chance to show God how good I could be, show Him that I was worth some reconsidering on His part, that maybe I deserved better than what I'd gotten so far on my most important day.

Lester looked mighty grateful when I stood up and walked toward the front of the bus, taking the first aid kit from him with a hiccup and an awkward, sorry smile. After all, Bobbi had been right when she'd said that this deep-fried pickle of a situation was all my fault. If it hadn't been for my birthday, or the choices I made *because* of my birthday, things might've turned out different. I was discovering that sometimes the outcome of a choice was almost as hard to predict or to control as a new savvy.

I opened the first aid kit as Lester tried in vain to cover the broken windows; three panes had blown out completely and a fourth looked ready to fall out of its frame at the first bump in the road. Lester appeared on the verge of tears himself as he finally gave up his attempts at wedging cardboard across the gaping holes and started the bus, the sound of the noisy engine doing little to dampen the voices still ringing in my head.

"That Lester . . ." said Rhonda.

"Stupid man . . ." said Carlene.

"She's not sure if she likes you, or if she thinks you're a freak," said Bobbi's angel, sounding bored.

"I'm not a freak, Bobbi," I said as I stubbornly pulled gauze and dried-up and useless antibacterial wipes from the first aid kit.

"What?" Bobbi cranked her neck around to look at me. "*What* did you just say?"

I swallowed hard and said nothing, realizing that I'd spoken out loud when I should have kept my mouth closed tight, tight, tight. I pulled a dusty cold pack from the first aid kit, the kind you have to twist to make go cold, and concentrated on that. I could feel Bobbi's eyes on me, trying to dissect me like a splayed and gutted frog. I twisted the pack with a *crack,* and felt a slow chill spread through the small plastic bag. Turning around, I moved three rows back to where Will Junior sat with his black eye.

The spring night air rushed through the broken windows as Lester took a turn too sharp and too fast, making the bus lurch and groan as he got us back onto the highway, sending boxes, magazines, and Bibles sliding. I stumbled and tumbled down onto the seat next to Will, handing him the cold pack for his eye with a little more force than I'd intended, nearly hitting him in the nose with it.

"Sorry," I said, trying to move quickly back into the aisle of the bumping, jumping bus. But Will Junior took hold of my hand and pulled me back down to sit on the seat next to him. He pressed the pack carefully to his eye, making a face. Still holding on to my hand, he looked at me full and square with his good eye.

"I'm not mad, Mibs," he said. I didn't know if he meant he wasn't mad about me pushing an icepack up his nose, or if he wasn't mad about the rest of it, about what had happened back in Bee. I was hoping it was that second thing.

"I'm not a freak," I said.

"I didn't say you were."

"No, but maybe you were thinking it."

Will paused, dropping the plastic pack to his lap, glancing at his sister, then studying me with both eyes as though trying to see all the way down to my DNA.

"Was Bobbi thinking it?"

"I have to clean up those scratches Bobbi gave Fish,"

I said, avoiding Will's question and starting to get up. But he held my hand tight.

"Was Bobbi thinking it? Was she thinking you're a freak?"

"Maybe."

"How do you know that, Mibs?"

I shrugged.

"How do you *know* that? Tell me, Mibs, what happened when you drew that picture on my hand? Why'd you flip out? And how does Fish make it storm like that? I know he's doing it—he's got to be." Will leaned in closer. "I just want to know . . ."

Will had that eager look on his face again. He was dying to know my secret.

"Just tell me, Mibs. Tell me what makes you Beaumonts so special."

WHAT DID MAKE MY FAMILY SO SPECIAL? All I knew was that being different ran through our veins. Grandpa had explained it to me years before, just after Grandma Dollop died, long before our move to Kansaska-Nebransas. Taking me with him to walk along the beach, he held my hand in his knobby one and told me how our family's extraordinary talents were passed down from our kin.

Grandpa had recounted stories about our ancestors, and of relations both close and distant. Since Beaumont was Poppa's name, Grandpa's stories held tales of Yeagers or Mendelssohns or Paynes, Danzingers, O'Connells, and Beachams. He spoke of cousins and aunts and nephews and nieces who had used their savvy to do good things, and of those who'd made a different choice—like Grandma Dollop's youngest sister, Jubilee, who could open any lock, and used her abilities to take things that didn't belong to her.

"A savvy's not a sickness or a disease, Mibs," Grandpa told me. "It's not magic or sorcery, either. Your savvy's in your blood. It's an inheritance, like your brown eyes or your grandma's long toes or her talent for dancing to polka music." Grandma Dollop had loved the oom-pah-pah sounds of polka music and had collected jars full before she died; Momma even had one or two of those jars left among the others on top of our kitchen cupboards in Kansaska-Nebransas. They were the ones Gypsy favored dancing to with all of her make-believe friends.

But talking about Grandma Dollop had ended Grandpa's storytelling that day on the beach. His memories of her were still too sharp and prickly with loss. If I wasn't careful of Grandpa's feelings, his grief would make the ground rumble, buckling the sidewalks and pushing the neighbor's lawn ornaments into the next yard over. I pretended not to notice the tears on Grandpa's cheeks as we walked on along the beach. But I held his hand tight and strong all the way back home.

Momma said that lots and lots of ordinary folk have a savvy, but most simply don't recognize it for what it is. "Some people know they feel different, Mibs," Momma told me. "But most don't know quite what makes them that way. One person might make strawberry jam so good that no one can get enough of it. Another might know just the right time to plant corn so that it's juicy and sweet as sugar on the hottest day of summer." Momma had laughed then, and I wasn't too sure if she was telling me the truth or pulling my leg. "There are even those folks who never get splashed by mud after a rainstorm or bit by a single mosquito in the summertime."

But as I grew up, I began to understand that a savvy is just a know-how of a different sort. Some people get called whiz kid or prodigy because they can do puzzles or play music better than anyone's supposed to, or they can recite the numbers of pi, 3.141592653 . . . on and on for hours from memory without a hitch. There are those who can run fast and win medals, and others who can talk anyone into buying anything at all. Those things are all just a special kind of know-how.

Well, we Beaumonts and our kin weren't so very different. We just had a name for our talents, and a fairly predictable time of life when our inheritance and our know-how kicked in and we had to learn to scumble—to use our savvy or work around it.

So, when Will Junior asked me, point-to-point-blank like a pellet from a BB gun, what made my family so special, I told him what my relations have been telling folk for generations when faced with questions that had to be answered.

"We Beaumonts are just like other people, Will." I said the words, halting and toneless from memory, like I was speaking the Pledge of Allegiance. "We get born, and sometime later we die. And in between, we're happy and sad, we feel love and we feel fear, we eat and we sleep and we hurt like everyone else."

"And?" he said, not letting me wriggle so easily off his pointed question mark of a hook.

"And . . . nothing. We've just got know-how of a different flavor than most."

"What's *your* 'know-how' then, Mibs?" he said, leaning toward me even closer.

"Well, she'd *better* know how to get me some Band-Aids pretty quick, if she knows what's good for her." Fish was standing over us, holding on to the backs of the seats to stay balanced and upright on the lurching, bouncing bus. He was looking at me like a storm cloud rising, his eyes full up with meaning. *Don't say anything* is what he was telling me. *Don't say anything!*

I glared at Fish. Caught between the two boys, and between my own fears of sharing and not sharing secrets, I shrugged my shoulders with a dismissive jerk. "There's nothing more I can tell you," I said at last, turning back to Will.

Family rules said: Keep quiet. No one told unless they had to, or unless they were getting married—starting families. It was always best to tell the one you're settling down with that your children may or may not develop the ability to walk through walls or to play the neighbor's piano from across the street without touching it.

Poppa had been in the navy, stationed down in Gulfport, Mississippi, when he met Momma at a Labor Day street carnival near the beach. Momma, just seventeen then, was visiting the coast with her older sister, Dinah. Our aunt Dinah wasn't perfect like Momma. Instead, she had a way of getting people to do whatever she said. With a word from Dinah, babies stopped crying. Surly teenage boys minded their manners and hugged their mothers. Even the stodgiest old codger would dance a jig if Dinah asked. Momma said that Aunt Dinah had stopped a bank robber once, just by telling him to sit down and be still until the police arrived. We all loved our aunt Dinah, but we were sure thankful that she wasn't *our* momma.

On that day of the street carnival, Poppa still knew nothing about savvy-folk like Momma and Dinah. He and his navy buddies were on leave and having a fine time strutting around in their sailor uniforms, whistling at all the girls. But the moment Poppa saw Momma, he was smitten; Poppa knew a perfect girl when he saw one.

They met at the ring toss game. Momma hadn't wanted to play, insisting to Dinah that it was hardly fair—she knew she could toss a ring onto a lurching, moving peg perfectly every time and didn't think it right to flaunt her savvy in such a public way, or in such a public place. Laughing, Dinah insisted Momma play—and that was that. Before long, Momma had a crowd of people watching her win the game again and again—a crowd that included Poppa and his buddies.

After watching Momma nail fifteen tosses in a row, Poppa had squeezed through the crowd, sidling right up to stand next to Momma.

"I'll tell you what," Poppa said jauntily into her ear,

rubbing his knuckles against his jaw. "If you make the next toss, I'll buy a ring and marry you." With a sly and knowing smile, Momma picked up another ring and took deliberate and careful aim. She sighted that peg and put a nice spin on that ring. The crowd went silent as the thin metal circle soared out toward the distant rows of shifting, jerking pegs . . . then fell short, clattering against the pegs and falling to the ground. Momma had missed, perfectly.

Momma raised one eyebrow and gave Poppa a not-too-sorry palms-up shrug. Dinah told Poppa to shove off in her savvy way, but Poppa just smiled. Poppa never had been one to give up easy, even up against the power of Aunt Dinah. In fact, Poppa never gave up on anything once he set his mind to it, and he told Momma so then and there.

The day Poppa asked Grandpa Bomba and Grandma Dollop for their blessing to marry Momma was the day he learned that some folks aren't exactly what you might expect. That was the day that Grandpa Bomba made

Poppa and Momma six acres of land on which to build a house—shifting all of their new neighbors east and west—and Grandma Dollop caught the young couple a love song in a jar so that they could listen to it whenever they liked. Momma and Poppa always kept that jar up on the mantel, loosening the lid now and again to let the never-ending song fill the house.

Listening to that song always lifted my spirits and I wished I had it with me as I sat there on that bus. Fish and Will were passing a fierce look back and forth like a football, and I worried that they might tackle each other again, right then and there. I was about to tell Fish to sit himself back down, when Lester hit the brakes. The big pink Bible bus heaved and shuddered like a whale caught by the tail, sending Fish sputtering and flailing onto his backside on the floor amidst an avalanche of Bibles and boxes. A horn sounded angrily as a car sped around us where we stood, stopped short in the middle of the dark rural highway.

Turning on the bus's flashing red lights, Lester leaned

on the lever that extended the bus's stop sign—stalling the few cars traveling on the same lonesome highway. Then he opened the squealing door, stood up without a single word or glance back in our direction, tucked his shirt down into his overalls, and walked off the bus.

FISH PICKED HIMSELF UP OFF THE floor and we all watched Lester climb down out of the bus, wondering what had made him grind to such a sudden halt. Fish, Bobbi, Will, and I all slid into the seats across the aisle in order to look out the cracked or missing windows and see what Lester was up to. I thought for a second that maybe Lester had pushed that bus past fifty-four miles per hour and we'd broken down, but when I saw him talking to a tall lady next to a car with its hood propped up and its hazard lights on, I knew that he'd only stopped to help.

The woman wore a long, coat-like, belted sweater that hung down past the hem of her old-fashioned green and white waitressing uniform. She was bigger and broader than Lester with his narrow chest and caved-in shoulders, and they made a funny pair standing there. Lester moved around the woman's car, then tinkered and fiddled under the open hood for a short time. Occasionally, a car edged around us despite the stop sign and the bus's flashing lights. When Lester finally stood upright, he shook his head and pointed back over his shoulder.

The woman contemplated the Heartland Bible Supply bus. When she saw our faces through the broken windows, she smiled like a small woman in a big woman's body and gave a little wave. Lester glanced up at us as well and his face split into a funny, unexpected grin, looking for all the world like, despite the bickering and fighting and the damage to his bus, the more was the merrier. I think that if Lester had had a tail it would have been wagging. Instead, he hooked his thumbs through the straps of his overalls and rocked back and forth on his heels.

The woman gave her broken-down clunker of a car one good, satisfying kick, then she allowed Lester to lead her up the three steep steps of the big pink bus, where he introduced her to us as though he'd just gotten hitched.

"Kids, this here's Miss Lill Kiteley and she'll b-be riding with us as far as Emerald."

We all looked from Lester to Lill to each other without a word. Fish shook his head and scowled. I knew what he was thinking, because I was thinking the same thing: One more adult to snoop in our business, and another delay to keep us from getting to Poppa. Lester's smile wavered and his right shoulder danced up near his ear as he registered our unhappiness at the sight of Lill. He cleared his throat and tugged on his loosened, crooked pink tie. The bus was silent. Well, *almost* silent.

"What do you know? Another stray . . ." Rhonda scorned from Lester's arm.

"Lester would take in a rabid hyena, even after it bit him," said Carlene from the other.

"You should know," grunted Rhonda.

"You've always been such an old witch, Rhonda," said Carlene in her most graveled tone.

"Well, it takes one to know one, I suppose," Rhonda snapped back.

"Hi," said Lill with another tiny little wave in our direction. "Are y'all Lester's kidlings?"

Bobbi snorted and moved back to her original seat with a halfhearted humph. "You've *got* to be kidding. I would rather have been raised by wolves."

"Naw," said Lester, hardly even hearing Bobbi. "These kids—"

"Are old friends of Lester's," I cut in before Lester could pronounce us stowaways. "I mean, he's a friend of the family. He's giving us a ride, right, Lester?"

Lester's smile skidded sideways and he scratched both sides of his head at once like that might jump-start his brain and help him keep up—as my quick interruption had caught him off guard. Lill looked back and forth from me to Lester, and I could tell she'd noticed Lester's confusion. But Lill didn't say anything, so I just grinned.

Another car honked at us, wanting to pass; the bus was still parked there on the highway with its flashers on and its stop sign extended. The added noise and pester fuddled Lester's brain even more and I felt ashamed at how easy it was to steer the deliveryman astray.

My own smile slipped away as I pointed back and forth between Fish and me. "Our poppa's in the hospital down in Salina," I said to Lill with a twist in my stomach. Lill, who was obviously quite a bit smarter than Lester, was looking at me carefully. "Mr. Swan was at my birthday party today," I continued, trying hard to keep looking the woman in the eye. "The party was at our *church in Hebron.*" I emphasized the last words to prompt Lester, but wasn't sure he was following my lead.

"Yeah," Bobbi broke in almost cheerily. "Good old Lester was talking to my father—he's the pastor there in Hebron—he was delivering some Bibles, and—"

"And when *our* dad"—Will pointed from Bobbi to himself, trying to help as well, but picking up the thread of deception with less delight than his sister—"well, when he found out that our good friend Lester here was headed back down to Salina—"

"He said that Lester should take us all with him," finished Fish in a flat and final tone, as though that was the end of it.

Lill looked at us all quizzically. I could tell she wasn't quite believing us. Lester, on the other hand, seemed somehow relieved, as though it suddenly all made much better sense to him why we were on board his bus, even if he didn't remember things in quite that way.

Lester did his best then to introduce us kids to Lill, since he was now a friend of the family and all. Unfortunately, he didn't do too well, calling Fish "Trout," and Will Junior "B-Bill Junior," and me "Midge." He got Bobbi's name right but forgot to mention Samson—or, maybe he hadn't remembered Samson hidey-holing it under the cot.

"It's nice to meet y'all," said Lill with a slow, suspicious drawl. Then she settled down sideways with her legs across the front seat of the bus near Lester, hanging her large white sneakers off the end of the bench like a kid herself, and keeping her back to the window so she could keep us all in sight.

As Lester pulled the stop sign back in and turned off the bus's flashing lights, Lill's eyes strayed to the scratches on Fish's face and to Will's black eye. "You all look like you need a wash and brush up. Are you sure this isn't the bus for the bad kids?" she said, eyeing the broken windows with a nervous laugh too small for her body.

"No, just the misfits," said Bobbi.

Lill smiled. "Then I should fit right in."

I'M NOT SURE EXACTLY WHAT IT was about Lill Kiteley, but I took to her right away. We all did. Even Bobbi seemed to thaw a bit—I caught her smiling once or twice as Lill yakked and joked around with us kids.

Lill was a lighthearted lady with no tattoos. She worked nights as a waitress in a truck-stop diner just off the interstate near Emerald and had been on her way to work when her rusted-out, dinted and dented, sorry excuse for a car gurgled and gargled and choked on its last drop of gasoline, then died. She had been sitting in her car by the side of the highway for nearly twenty minutes, contemplating sticking her thumb out to hitch the twenty-five-mile stretch between where she was and where she needed to be, when Lester Swan saw her and stopped the bus. Now, as the bus jounced on down the highway toward the interstate, Lill moved to help me clean up Fish's face, never even asking what had happened.

Lester was having trouble keeping his eyes off Lill and on the road where they belonged. Every now and again, someone in another car would lay on their horn like a shout when Lester drifted out of his lane and into theirs as he twisted his head to glance Lill's way.

With Lill there, it was almost like having a momma on the bus. She fussed over each of us in turn, cleaning and bandaging Fish's cheek and checking Will's eye.

"Here, let me fix this up for you, kidling," Lill said to me as she tugged gently at the purple ribbons of the flower on my special-occasion dress, unpinning and repinning the ribbons higher up on my shoulder. That silky flower had become rumpled and off-kilter from the day's ruckus, and my dress was now dirty and wrinkled.

"This is a mighty fine dress you've got on," continued Lill, still concentrating on the ribbons.

"My poppa picked it out all by himself," I told her, remembering the contented look on Poppa's face as I'd danced that dress around the living room. I smiled to myself at the memory, then faltered as my lips began to tremble.

As we drove on and on through the dark, I told Lill at length about my poppa and how he'd bought me my dress, not giving up until he'd found me just the one—how he'd handed it to me in a big white box tied shut with stretchy gold elastic that made it feel extra-special. My heart ached as I told her about the World's Largest Porch Swing, and about the accident on the highway and the cars stacked up like Sunday pancakes. Then I told her about Momma and Rocket and how they were already there, already with Poppa at Salina Hope Hospital. Lill listened to my whole story without interrupting once. But her face showed me that she was hearing every word, as her expression changed from a warm smile to a laugh, to kind and sympathetic concern.

"My poppa needs me," I said at last, more to myself than to Lill. "He needs me to get down there to Salina. He's like Sleeping Beauty and I have to wake him up."

I ignored Lill's unmistakable look of worry as I said this. I knew she believed that I was getting my hopes up to think that I had the power to do anything to help Poppa. But she was wrong, so I ignored her. I ignored her like I ignored all of the voices in my head—the ones that were supposed to be there, and the ones that weren't. I would figure those out later, after Poppa was back home and better. I had no time for listening now.

"Your poppa sounds like a very nice poppa, kidling," said Lill softly. "And that's a very spiffy dress." That made me feel proud at first. Then, looking down at the yellow fabric and the white rickrack striping, I couldn't help becoming self-conscious as I remembered how the girls at the church had laughed at it.

"Yeah, I guess." I shrugged, feeling low for my

embarrassment, like somehow I was disappointing Poppa by doubting the special-ness of my special-occasion dress. After a pause and a quick glance at Bobbi, I said, "You don't think this dress makes me look too much like a little girl, do you?"

Lill gave me a curious look. "Does it make you *feel* like a little girl?" she asked quietly.

"Only when I'm around Bobbi. She's sixteen," I said by way of explaining. Lill's face broke into a broad smile as she too looked Bobbi's way.

"You know, that Bobbi makes me feel a bit like a little girl too," Lill said with a laugh. "But I'll tell you a secret about sixteen," she continued, bending down to whisper in my ear. "Sixteen can feel older and scarier than forty-two, which is what I am. I think Bobbi's just feeling sharp-edged right now, so don't you mind her. Your dress is perfect."

That made me feel better. I smoothed out the wrinkles that had become pressed into its skirt since I'd put the dress on back in Kansaska-Nebransas, overly conscious of the fact that Will was watching me.

Lill looked from me to Will knowingly. "Well, isn't that boy of yours just the tomcat's kitten?" she said with a smile, nudging me with her elbow.

"What? Will's not— He's just— He's not—" I stammered in protest, feeling my cheeks burn.

"That boy can't stop staring, and I know he's not looking at me. It's plain to see Will's sweet on you," Lill continued with a small laugh, patting my leg in a way that made me feel as though she and I had been friends for a long, long time. "You see, Mibs? You're not such a little girl. You've already got a handsome boy looking your way."

I sealed my mouth shut at that. I remembered the way Ashley Bing had kept her eyes glued on Will back at the church in Hebron. I also remembered the way I hadn't liked her doing it. I could imagine Ashley's voice in my head, "Missy-pissy's got herself a *boyfriend,*" with Emma Flint echoing, "A *boyfriend!*"

"Don't fret it, kidling," said Lill. "Trust me, in a few more years Will Junior will be the least of your worries."

Lill put an arm around my shoulders and squeezed me to her just as Momma would have done. For a minute I thought maybe Lill might be an angel sent to look after us as we bumped our way along the highway in that big pink Bible bus—not a devil-tailed angel like Bobbi's tattoo, nor a heavily perfumed and sappy-smiling angel like the air freshener hanging in the front window of Miss Rosemary's minivan. A real angel. One with really big feet.

SOMETIME LATER, SAMSON THE SHADOW APPEARED soundlessly next to Fish, just as we were nearing the town of Emerald. He was clutching the empty potato chip bag. The blinking yellow lights of cross-street traffic signals lit Lill's eyes as they widened in surprise and she looked at me questioningly, pointing at Samson where he sat whispering to Fish.

"And who is this critter?" Lill asked in a hushed tone, like he was a shy, wild thing come out of hiding.

"That's another one of my brothers. His name is Samson," I explained. "He's seven and he doesn't talk too much."

"The strong, silent type, eh? Hello, Samson," Lill said kindly. Samson looked at Lill impassively, the way the animals look back at you when you are watching them at the zoo. Then he shot his eyes again to Fish, nudging his thin elbow into Fish's ribs and crackling the empty bag.

"My brother's hungry, ma'am," Fish explained. "We haven't eaten much of anything since lunchtime, and it must be well past supper by now."

Lill looked at her wristwatch, holding it up close to her face in the dim light of the bus. She breathed a heavy sigh. "You're sure right about that, Mr. Fish. It's long past supper and long, long past the start of my shift at the diner. If there's one thing I've got a knack for—a true talent even—that's being late." She looked around at all of us and her eyes crinkled with a sad and regretful smile. Her initial distrust of us seemed to melt away as I'd told her stories about Poppa and the accident. As I'd spoken, unable to hide the waves of fear and sorrow that rolled through me, Lill responded with sympathy.

I imagined there was nothing like a heartsick girl with a sad story to win over a softhearted lady.

"But I'll tell y'all this," Lill continued. "If I get to work and find I still have myself a job, if my boss doesn't fire me on the spot for being so late—late *again,"* she groaned, "I'll see that y'all get a fine supper. I'll even make sure you each get a slice of pie before you're on your way again—my treat."

"Do you have banana cream?"

Everyone turned to look at Samson, surprised to hear him speak above a whisper. His choir-boy voice was husky from disuse and under-cot dust, but still sweet as ever. I tried to remember the last time I'd heard him say anything out loud—a day? a week? a month? That was just the way it was with my broody brother. I smiled at Samson now; I never knew he liked banana cream pie.

"Oh goodie, he speaks," muttered Bobbi. And with Samson still sitting stone-faced and solemn, a grinning giggle spread through the ranks, turning into a gut-busting crackup as the day's tension released like waves hitting shore. If I could have forgotten about why I was where I was, I might almost have been happy. Despite the mayhem, for the first time, I felt like I might be making friends—and that even included Bobbi.

Lester followed Lill's directions into the town of Emerald. The Emerald Truck Stop Diner and Lounge was on the far edge of town, lit up in weak green neon. Bright white fluorescent light cut through the darkness, spilling out through the glass door at the front of the restaurant. There were some rough and tough-looking motorcycles parked near the road. The parking lot was full of pickup trucks, and semitrailers were lined up like side-by-side train cars in a lot behind the building. Lester had to park the big pink Bible bus past all of these trucks and trailers in a back alley that was cluttered with smelly Dumpsters, stacks of splintered wooden pallets, and old, rotting cardboard boxes.

"I s'pose I c-could have let you all off up front," Lester said apologetically, helping Lill down off the bus like she was a princess.

"Just stick close, kidlings," said Lill, looking around the poorly lit alleyway. The rest of us climbed down from the bus behind the two adults, stepping past newspapers and torn sheets of dirty industrial plastic that rustled and snapped in the evening breeze. Whether or not the breeze was a normal earthly breeze or the result of Fish's concern for Poppa, I couldn't say; his face was unreadable as we marched down the deserted alley.

Lill took Samson's hand and he walked between her and Lester without complaint, as though it was something he did every day. I was surprised to see Samson take so quickly to strangers. Though, from the set of his jaw and the stiff way he held his body, I knew that he too was scared and missing Momma and Poppa, and that right now Lill and Lester were the next best thing. Fish walked out ahead of everyone, like a scout making sure the way was safe; Bobbi tramped behind, and Will and I brought up the rear.

That's when I saw something that made me jump nearly out of my skin. I stopped on the edge of the parking lot behind the Emerald Truck Stop where the alley fed out into the street. Past a rank Dumpster surrounded by mounds of overstuffed trash bags, a dirty hand was sticking out from under what looked like a pile of old clothes. The hand lay palm up, fingers outstretched like it was reaching out to me for help.

I grabbed Will's arm and jerked him back toward me, hardly daring to breathe. The others walked ahead, not noticing the grimy hand or Will and me dropping behind to stare at it and the body of the man it was attached to. I looked at Will and he looked back at me, eyes round in the eerie light from the single nearby streetlamp.

Looking closer, we saw the still, prone form of an old homeless man, whiskered and filthy and stinking of drink and despair. Will tried to pull me away. He nodded toward several empty bottles scattered on the ground next to the man. "There's nothing we can do for him, Mibs," he said, sorry but firm like a police officer directing onlookers away from an accident. "Come on, Mibs, let's go." He pulled gently on my arm again, but I didn't budge.

"What if he's dead?" I said in a whisper. My heart was pounding. Watching the man just lying there on the pavement, I couldn't help but think about Poppa lying just as still and lifeless down in Salina, and my heart came close to bursting.

"The guy probably just drank too much and passed out, Mibs," Will said nervously, not wanting to linger any longer, wanting to go and catch up to the others. But I was hardly listening anymore, hardly feeling the touch of Will's hand on my arm. All I could see was that unfortunate man. All I could think was that maybe there *was* something I could do to help him. I could wake him up. I could wake him up the same way I was going to wake up Poppa when I got down to Salina. No more silly voices in my head, it was time for my true savvy to kick in like it should. It had to happen now.

I took a step toward the lifeless lump of flesh that had once been a walking, talking, hoping, dreaming man—once been someone's son or friend . . . or father.

"Mibs!" Will hissed my name and tried to pull me back, but I shook him off.

I knelt down on the pavement, barely feeling the gravel that dug into my knee. I got just close enough to reach my own hand out and place one timid, shaking finger on the inside of the prone man's upturned wrist, as though I was trying to feel for his pulse.

I dug down deep into myself, searching for that thing, that spark, that powerful storm all my own—searching for the wellspring of my own savvy strength and concentrating with all my might on waking up the man on the ground in front of me.

Wake up.

Wake up.

Please. Wake up.

I thought it over and over in my head, whispering

it like a chant just under my breath. I thought it harder than any thought I'd ever thought before. I concentrated so hard that my eyes began to water and my teeth ached from grinding them together.

My finger pressed harder and harder against the cold, bony wrist. I could feel the slow, almost hesitant pulse of blood beneath his skin. For a minute, nothing happened. Then a harsh and hollering voice blasted through my head, sending me backward and scrabbling against the pavement.

"Don't want to see any more . . . feel any more. Just let me fade away . . . I've seen too much . . . too much!"

The voice in my head was filled with the undertow of bottomless despair. I felt the unconscious man's ache and anguish just behind my eyes, rattling my brain like concussions of shrapnel.

"Seen too much! Leave me alone . . ." But the man didn't wake up.

I couldn't wake him up.

That's when I knew—then and there and sure as

sure—that's when I knew that there wasn't anything—*anything*—I could do to help Poppa.

I felt as though someone had punched me in the stomach and pulled out all my bones, turning me into a queasy, useless blob of Jell-O. The ruined man shifted on the ground without waking, turning his hand over to expose a dull tattoo of a soaring eagle inked years ago on the back of his hand. As I listened to the distress and despair of the voice crying out inside my head, that eagle flapped and screeched and beat its wings as if gone mad, like all it wanted was to break free and fly away.

I realized then that it had been coincidence, not my savvy, that had woken Gypsy up that morning, and that Samson's dead pet turtle had played a trick on me, merely come out of its long hibernation on this most important day with no regard for savvies or hopings or misunderstandings. Nature simply did what nature does, and I mixed that up with me.

For the very first time since I was old enough to

know what it meant to have a savvy, since the day that I'd begun to dream of what my own talent might come to be, I wished that I was more like Poppa and had no savvy at all. No savvy to cause me heartache. No savvy to make me hope, and then leave me useless.

"COME ON, MIBS," SAID WILL QUIETLY, helping me up off the ground and brushing the dirt and gravel from my hands. "Let's go. Everyone's waiting for us." He turned me away from the unconscious man. But Will didn't know what I'd heard. He didn't know what I'd seen. He could turn away easier than I could because he didn't have to listen. Weak-kneed and shaken, it seemed impossible for me to walk away. Yet when Will took hold of my elbow awkwardly, I allowed him to lead me toward the glow of the Emerald Truck Stop Diner and Lounge.

The others were waiting at the front of the restaurant. Lester held the door open for each of us as we entered. Inside the diner, there were so many people you couldn't stir them with a stick, and I understood bitterly exactly how wrong Rocket had been when he'd said that girls only got the quiet, polite savvies. Noise, noise, noise was all I'd gotten; when I stepped into that diner it was most definitely not *quiet,* and some of the voices and thoughts jangling in my ears were far from polite.

Walking into a diner full of tattooed bikers and truckers made me feel like someone had switched on a razzmatazz radio inside my head—a radio with a dial that kept spinning with a fizz and a zing from station to station to station to station without stop. Still reeling from my encounter with the homeless man, the new, added onslaught of all these strangers' thoughts and feelings and questions and answers made me feel like I was going to be sick.

A wave of dizziness hit me, making the room lurch, and I stumbled, uselessly covering my ears and trying to stay upright. Fish caught me on one side as Will grabbed me on the other, each boy glaring at the other, both trying to steady me and keep me on my feet.

"Ah, geez—" said Lester, sticking his hands in his pockets and taking a step back, none too sure what to do about falling-down girls.

"You okay, honey?" Lill said to me, turning around and reaching out to help. She was ignoring a lady in a green and white uniform that matched her own. The other woman had red hair and a surly glower, and was trying to push pitchers of coffee and water Lill's way, complaining like a wet cat about Lill being late.

"I think my sister was just on that bus too long," Fish told Lill, nervous and hasty. Fish was trying to cover for me and my savvy, even though he was still unsure what exactly he was covering for. I was grateful to my brother, and ashamed. I knew that I was going to have to tell him everything: about the voices, and about how I'd gotten us all into this big mess for nothing.

"Well, maybe Mibs should lie down in the back room for a spell," said Lill. In several quick long strides that the rest of us had to hop to keep up with, she led us past the piping and bellyaching of the red-haired waitress, past booths and tables filled with diners and their deafening thoughts. Lill led us past a long counter where customers sat perched atop round spinning stools, eating their onion rings and drinking coffee, and took us through an Employee's Only door next to the kitchen.

We found ourselves in a cramped storeroom that smelled like ketchup and pickles and mustard. Lill shrugged out of her sweater and hung it on a coatrack inside the door. Shelves stacked high with bread rolls, jars of mayonnaise, and enormous cans of beans and tomatoes lined the room, reminding me of our basement back in Mississippi and all of Grandma Dollop's noisy jars. Filing cabinets, a cluttered desk, and a battered sofa filled the only area without supply shelves. A pile of newspapers lay on the floor near a back door labeled *Emergency Exit* and there was a low table in front of the sofa littered with crumbs and empty soda cans.

A small black-and-white television sat on top of one

of the filing cabinets, its antenna aslant and festooned with bows of crumpled aluminum foil. The TV was turned on, its poor, snowy image broadcasting the evening news. A newscaster was reporting from somewhere in Kansas, covering a story about freak power outages and damaged electrical grids that ran up and down Highway 81 on most of its path through Kansas and into the town of Salina. Fish and I exchanged knowing glances, fairly confident that Rocket had something to do with those problems.

Lill told Fish and Will to get me to rest on the sofa as she turned the volume down on the little TV, but I brushed off their orders like annoying, buzzing flies. Just being in the back room helped. My head still hurt something awful and my stomach still wanted to jump and jive and do the twist. I could still hear all the voices, but tucked back in the storeroom as I was, those voices were muted low now like the TV. I sat on the edge of the frayed sofa cushions, staring at the floor and trying not to listen—trying to let all sounds, both inside and outside of my head, blend together into one endless, punishing roar, as I mourned the loss of my hopes for my savvy—and for my poppa.

"She just needs a little space," I heard Fish tell the others above the din in my head.

"I *really* have to get to work," said Lill apologetically, linking her hand through Lester's arm where he stood next to her. "I may be in luck tonight, y'all. I didn't see The Great and Powerful Ozzie when we came in." She sounded relieved and laughed her small laugh, bumping Lester with her hip and nearly knocking him to the ground.

"Ozzie's the manager here and he'd put a knot in my tail if he caught me coming in at this hour. Mr. Fish, why don't you stay with your sister and I'll have the others bring you kidlings something to eat in a wink and a shake." Fish just nodded without looking away from me. Lill pulled Lester back out into the restaurant, and Bobbi and Will Junior followed after, Will casting a long worried look over his shoulder, obviously reluctant to leave my side. I looked around for Samson.

"Where's—?" I started.

"Who knows," said Fish with a shrug. "Y'know Samson. He'll turn up." Pushing aside the empty soda cans and brushing off some of the crumbs, Fish sat down on the low table directly in front of me and, patience worn thin, crossed his arms over his chest. "Tell me."

Fish wanted the full hokeypokey on my savvy. He wanted details. He wanted them *now*.

Needing to look anywhere besides my brother's sullen face, I stared at the fuzzy images on the small TV screen across the room; there was so much static that it was like trying to watch television through soda pop bubbles; the sound was too low to hear. The story about the power outages ended and the anchorman behind the news desk swiveled his chair to a new, more dramatic angle, looking doubly serious. A telephone number began marching herky-jerky across the bottom of the screen as the anchorman moved his lips mutely.

I didn't know quite what to tell Fish. I had been so sure about my savvy. We wouldn't have been sitting there in the storeroom of the Emerald Truck Stop Diner and Lounge if I hadn't been positive that I could bring Poppa back home to us, back home to Kansaska-Nebransas. But it was now as clear as Momma's don't-touch-or-else crystal that my savvy had different plans for me, and I was nothing but sorry and filled up with misery and dread at the thought of telling my brother.

"It's the ink, Fish," I finally said, still finding it easier to focus on the black-and-white fizz of the news report than to look my brother in the eye.

"What ink, Mibs?" said Fish.

"Any ink, I think, as long as it's on someone's skin."

Fish squinted at me. "Go on."

I didn't know how to explain. I didn't want to rummage through my mind for the right words and try to put them into the right sentences like the pieces of a jigsaw puzzle. It felt too hard. I was tired and I was hungry. And, now that I knew there was nothing, nothing, nothing I could do to help Poppa, I just wanted to go home. Home to Grandpa Bomba and home to

Gypsy. Home to the mud left behind by Fish's rain. Home to be homeschooled and grow moss in pickle jars and learn how to scumble this savvy and make it know its place.

"*Tell* me, Mibs," Fish demanded. I tore my eyes away from the little TV, where a reporter was interviewing a man and a woman who looked, through the sleety static of the poor reception, a little like Pastor Meeks and Miss Rosemary. I met my brother's stare and sighed again.

"Maybe I should just show you." I pulled the silver pen Will Junior had given me for my birthday from the pocket of my skirt. "Hold out your hand and think of a number—any number. But make it a hard one."

Fish drew his eyebrows together, looking wary. "What are you going to do, Mibs?"

"It's not a hurricane, Fish," I said impatiently. "It's not dynamite. Trust me." Fish thrust his hand toward me stiffly, his lips pressed together into a tight, straight line. I could tell I'd made him mad—my hair blew back from my face and the newspapers by the door rustled and fluttered. I placed the tip of the pen to the skin of Fish's palm, and then stopped.

"Are you thinking of a number?" I asked him sharply. "Because I don't want to hear *anything* but a number." The last thing I wanted was to hear what was going on inside my own brother's head. I shivered. Gross.

Fish squinted at me again and nodded, all curt and serious and grumpy. "I've got a number."

"Just think it to yourself over and over," I said, and I pressed the pen down to draw a small quick circle punctuated with the eyes and mouth of a smiley face that wasn't smiling so much as *not* smiling. The mouth of the face rippled like a grimace and the eyes blinked twice.

"Two thousand, two hundred twenty-two and a half," it said. *"Two thousand, two hundred twenty-two and a half . . . Two thousand, two hundred—"*

I spit quick on Fish's hand and smeared the face away before Fish's thoughts had the chance to wander somewhere else. Fish didn't move, but just sat looking at me like I was some kind of a whack-of-a-quack fortune-teller at the county fair, reading his palm and telling him how many squalling, bawling children he was going to have when he was grown up.

"Two thousand, two hundred twenty-two and a half," I repeated. "Right?"

Fish gave me a hard-boiled nod, looking grave but unruffled. "You can hear what I'm thinking?"

"Thinking or feeling, I guess."

"So you read minds, do you?" A singsong voice broke out above the droning roar and hummed inside my head.

Bobbi was standing just inside the storeroom, looking as though she was about to drop her armful of plastic baskets all overflowing with burgers and fries.

"So you read minds, do you?"

BOBBI LOOKED AT ME AND FISH. She'd seen and heard everything.

"I knew it. I *knew* it," she said, setting the burger baskets down on the desk and backing up the few feet toward the door. "I knew there was something mental about you. Will's never going to believe this." Bobbi left the storeroom before Fish or I could say a word.

Fish leaped up from his seat on the low table. "I've got to stop her!"

"There's nothing you can do, Fish," I said, jumping up from the sofa to grab my brother's arm, to keep him from doing something stupid. But there was no need. Fish halted dead in his tracks, staring at the little television on top of the filing cabinet.

I followed his gaze and inhaled sharply. There, in all the snowy black-and-white importance such a tiny TV could muster, our photographs—Bobbi's, Will's, Fish's, Samson's, and mine—began flashing across the screen with ALERT! MISSING! ALERT! scrolling across the bottom of the screen, along with an eight-hundred number to call if anyone had seen us.

We watched our pictures flick and wobble through the poor reception of the small TV, then the newscast cut over to another reporter interviewing the pastor and his wife in front of the church. Miss Rosemary looked sorrowful and worried; Pastor Meeks looked stiff and strained and spitting mad.

Fish clenched his jaw, his muscles tense. "We've got big problems, Mibs," he muttered without looking away from the television.

I glanced from the television to the door leading into the dining area and swallowed hard, trying to imagine what else could go wrong that day. Things had already gone from bad to worse, and I had a feeling our situation wasn't going to be getting better any time soon.

Just as Fish reached out his hand to turn off the television, the back door emergency exit burst open with the loud rasp of metal on metal, startling me and Fish so badly we both jumped back. A barrel-chested man in a hooded sweatshirt and green spandex shorts scowled at us from the doorway. He had a gold chain around his neck and a large gold-nugget ring on each hand.

This had to be Ozzie, manager of the Emerald Truck Stop Diner and Lounge. He pulled a toothpick from between his lips and flicked it back over his shoulder toward the parking lot. Then he stepped inside, bearing down on Fish and me like an angry bison.

"What are you kids doing back here?" he demanded, his breath a loud mix of bluster and buffalo wings. "Can't you read? This area is for employees only. Beat it. Scram." Ozzie advanced, waving his hands at us like a muscled wizard shooing chickens. "Go find your parents, or go play with the jukebox or something."

"We're here with Lill," I squeaked as he pushed us backward toward the door to the dining area. "She said we could be in here." But that didn't stop Ozzie's forward momentum. In fact, it only made things worse.

"BWAAAAAP!" he said, making a harsh and showy sound like a game show buzzer. "Wrong answer! Lill's at the top of my list right now. In fact, Lill's about to get canned." With that, Ozzie pressed Fish and me right out of the storeroom.

Pushed back into the middle of all those chaotic, noisy voices, I tried my best to keep from becoming discombobulated, tried to figure out how to scumble those thunderous thoughts that didn't belong to me, but that was a hard thing, a thing that could take years—horrible long years of this stupid savvy—and I had no idea how to do it.

I stayed as close to the edge of the room as I could, hovering near the wall closest to the kitchen, next to the long dining counter. I was aware of the sound of plates hitting plates in the kitchen, the sound of silverware hitting the floor, and the pop and sizzle of frying burgers. But all the boisterous voices in my head floated on top of those other ordinary sounds like warring battleships on a churning ocean.

I couldn't tell if the room was spinning or if *I* was, and the scene that followed flew by me like a series of snapshots set to the jingle-jangle jumble of other people's thoughts and feelings.

When Ozzie entered the dining room, Lill was behind the counter with three pies lined up in front of her, putting the first slice into the banana cream with a long, wedge-shaped pie knife. Lester sat near her on a round stool, biting into a thick burger and spilling yellow mustard onto his twisted tie.

"Bobbi's with Will Junior over by the jukebox," I heard Fish say into my ear. Looking toward the corner of the room, I saw Bobbi talking to Will and pointing our way.

"She's telling him everything," said Fish darkly. I

noticed Will looking back and forth from his sister to me, but at that point my head hurt too much to care about his reaction. And by then, Ozzie had started yelling again.

Ozzie stepped over to Lill, picking up the banana cream pie and taking the knife out of her hands.

"That's it for you, Lill," Ozzie said, waving the pie knife covered in whipped cream through the air as he spoke, gesturing wildly and hitting Lester on the head with a stray slice of banana. "You've tried my patience too far. You may be a decent waitress—when you manage to get yourself here on time—but I've had it. This is the last time you show up late and the last time you slice pie at the Emerald Truck Stop Diner."

"But, Ozzie—" Lill started to protest.

"I want you out of here right now, Lill Kiteley!" shouted Ozzie in his spandex shorts, obviously enjoying the sound of his own voice and the attention it brought him from the red-haired waitress. By now everyone in the diner had stopped talking and turned to watch the scene unfolding between Ozzie and Lill. Even the song on the jukebox ended, as if it too were listening in. Lester dropped his hamburger and slowly wiped the banana from his thinning hair. Will and Bobbi stepped closer to the counter, but stopped when they saw Ozzie wielding the knife. With everyone's attention fixed and focused on The Great and Powerful Ozzie, even the voices in my head grew quiet.

Still holding the pie, as though he didn't trust Lill enough to put it down near her, Ozzie set the knife into a tub beneath the counter. Watching him, I saw Samson sitting still and quiet under the counter in an open space just next to the dish tub, so dark and shadowy that Ozzie hadn't even noticed him.

"Ozzie, just let me—" Lill tried again to speak.

"BWAAAAAP!" Ozzie made the same annoying game show noise, cutting Lill off. "You lose, Lill!"

Ozzie turned, holding the pie in his left hand; with his right hand, he opened the cash register. He pulled out a wad of bills and made a production out of throwing the money at Lill, who, for all the world, looked like she might melt away into a flood of tears, should she lose control and let the dam burst.

"There," said Ozzie, as the bills fell to the floor at Lill's big feet. "You can pick up your consolation prize—that should cover your last paycheck."

I could see the red-haired waitress smirk as Lill, with all the dignity she could muster, bent down to pick the money up off the floor.

It would have been better for everyone if Ozzie had managed to maintain a little more restraint. When Ozzie started laughing cruel as cruel at poor Lill, now down on the floor picking up her final pay, the real unbridled brouhaha began.

"Mister," said Lester, slamming his fist against the counter as his twitch worked his shoulder up and down like one of the pistons inside the engine of his bus. "That's no way to treat a lady." Saying this, Lester shoved his plate aside and stood up, walking around the counter to help Lill gather her money.

At the very same moment, Samson leaned forward from his hidey-hole behind the counter and bit The Great and Powerful Ozzie hard on the leg.

Ozzie shrieked like a little girl and the banana cream pie flew out of his hands to land upside down with a sickening *splump* on the floor in front of him.

"Why you little—!" Clutching his leg and hopping on one foot, Ozzie pulled the pie knife back out of the tub menacingly.

"No!" I cried out.

Seeing Samson pop up from behind the counter within easy reach of the angry man and his pie knife, Bobbi and Will rushed across the floor of the diner. They both tried to grab for the knife over the countertop as Samson shot out from behind it, running toward the storeroom. Fish and I charged forward and together we shoved Ozzie hard in the middle of his muscled back, sending him lurching forward and slip-sliding through the fallen pie. The burly man skated on one foot through bananas and custard as Fish's angry wind swept through the diner, unbalancing Ozzie even further. Ozzie toppled backward with a thud.

The red-haired waitress screamed and customers rose to their feet, unsure if they should help or even whose side they should be on if they did.

"Let's get out of here!" Bobbi shouted, sprinting around the counter to help Lill and Lester collect the rest of the money. Then she and Will Junior herded the rooted and rattled adults past the cursing, floundering Ozzie and back toward the Employees Only door for an emergency escape out the emergency exit door, Fish and I wasting no time in following.

Passing through the storeroom, Lill grabbed her sweater from its peg and looked at the rest of us, shaking her head. Her face was red and she had pie on her big white shoes.

"Sorry all," Lill said breathlessly as we headed toward the door. "Looks like we bad kids and misfits got to hit the road again." She pointed toward the baskets sitting on the desk where Bobbi had set them earlier.

"Grab those burgers, kidlings. You can eat on the bus." Lill looked down at Samson, who had taken her hand, looking mournful. "Sorry about the banana cream, critter," Lill said with earnest. Lester stopped short.

"Everyone just hold on one minute." Lester's decisive tone stopped us in our tracks. Without even pausing to twitch, he hoisted one finger into the air like a signal to charge, then turned and pushed back through the door to the dining area. For a moment, I thought Lester had blown his last fuse and had run the wrong way by mistake. But a moment later, he was back with a second cream pie held high above his head like a trophy. He barreled across the room in a hot-footed hustle toward the exit, as Lill gave the battered sofa in the storeroom one firm and final kick, just as she'd done to her broken-down car. Then she pushed the rest of us after Lester, all tumbling out the back door into the parking lot behind the restaurant, away from Ozzie and the Emerald Truck Stop Diner and Lounge.

Chapter 20

AS WE RUSHED OUT INTO THE spring night, the air was crisp and cool, laced with the smell of diesel fumes and chicken fingers. After the noisy babble and bedlam inside the restaurant, being outside was a relief, a soothing hush of sky and pavement. I could hear cars on the road in front of the diner, each sounding like nothing more than a wave lapping shore.

Nobody spoke as we hopped quickly over potholes in the light of the single streetlamp, weaving in and out of trucks and semitrailers toward the distant corner of the lot, moving toward the alley. We kept a close eye behind us in case Ozzie or anyone else might be giving chase. But whether he was still lying on his back in the middle of the remains of banana cream pie, or just too embarrassed to follow, it didn't appear that Ozzie was coming after us.

During all the commotion inside the restaurant, I'd forgotten about the down-and-out man by the Dumpster. We had nearly passed him again before the noisy return of *"Seen too much . . ."* would not allow me to forget that he was still there. I felt the pinch of sorrow and remorse, and realized that while my savvy had done nothing to help the soul-sick, broken man, there was something else that I *could* do for him. Dropping behind the others, I set my burger basket down on the ground near the outstretched hand. Then I removed the purple ribbon flower pinned to the shoulder of my special-occasion dress and set that down beside the burger, feeling sure that Poppa would understand. Aside from my silver pen, it was the only thing I had to give, the only way I had to show the man that I'd seen him. That I'd listened.

Heading back to the bus, everyone was so breathless and shaken by the incident inside the diner, only Will seemed to take any notice of my tiny offering, giving me a warm look as he waited for me to catch up.

Farther now from the crowd of voices inside the restaurant and the voice of the homeless man, I was disappointed, but not surprised, when Bobbi and Carlene and Rhonda all rolled back into my head as loud and rowdy as if they owned the place.

"Lester's got his foot stuck in a deep bucket of mud now . . ."

"The man sure has a way of doing it."

As Lester struggled to open the door of the bus and balance the stolen pie at the same time, the rest of us leaned up against the side of the bus to catch our breath. Despite everything that had just happened, Bobbi was staring at me almost calmly, arms folded, with a probing, yet guarded, look on her face. Will Junior stood behind her, his expression unreadable.

"Tell me what I'm thinking. Do you know what I'm

thinking?" that little angel on Bobbi's back sang through my brain. Carlene's and Rhonda's voices took backstage to Bobbi's angel, their never-ending Lester-bashing sounding like backup vocals to Bobbi's newest tune.

"Tell me what I'm thinking. Do you know what I'm thinking?" Bobbi pushed her thoughts at me, louder and louder.

"Tell me what I'm thinking. Do you know what I'm thinking?

"Tell me what I'm thinking. Do you know what I'm thinking?"

She was driving me crazy. As Lester finally got the door open, I put my fingers in my ears and started to hum "The Star-Spangled Banner" just as loud as anyone can hum. But Fish spun me around, pulling my finger out of my right ear, and whispering tightly, "What are you hearing, Mibs?"

"Bobbi's got herself a tattoo on her back and it won't stop yammering at me," I whispered back. "She *knows,* Fish, remember?"

Fish threw a glance Bobbi's way. The girl was leaning up against the side of the bus watching me like I was a mouse and she was a cat—a cat who liked playing with its food before eating. Will Junior was standing just a bit behind her, his face screwed up now as though trying to decide if he understood the punch line of a joke. Bobbi didn't look at Fish; she was too busy burning her eyes right into me.

"Tell me what I'm thinking. Do you know what I'm thinking?

"Tell me what I'm thinking. Do you know what I'm thinking?"

"Stop it, Bobbi," said Fish, one hand raised in a tight fist, as Lester and Lill climbed up into the bus with Samson.

"Stop what?" said Bobbi, overflowing with fake flibbertigibbety sugar.

"You know what," said Fish, angrily throwing his burger onto the ground. A gust of wind blew Bobbi's hair up around her head in a flurry, and the air turned humid and hot. Bobbi stopped leaning against the bus and stood up straight. Narrowing her eyes across the light from the streetlamp at Fish, and spitting at strands of hair caught in her gum, Bobbi threw down her own burger, as though accepting a challenge to fight.

"I'm just *thinking*. Do you want me to stop *thinking?*"

Fish's next gust was stronger, blowing Bobbi's hair straight back and plastering her clothes to her body as though she were facing straight into a tempest. Will Junior took a step back and turned to shield his eyes—and his burger—as dirt and gravel, lifted from the crumbling pavement by the strength of Fish's wind, swept toward him and Bobbi. Ragged shreds of plastic sheeting whipped and snapped along the alleyway like a multitude of wild, ghostly specters. From out of nowhere came a spatter of biting rain that hit the side of the bus with the sound of a sprinkler hitting a chain-link fence.

Fish was standing in front of me now, acting like a shield between me and Will and Bobbi Meeks. He had his feet planted and his arms out at his sides like some kind of comic book Superkid, his own hair whipping up a frenzy as he pushed out powerful storms of wind and rain that started the bus rocking and knocked Bobbi backward into Will.

Lester poked his head out the door of the bus, his combed-over hair flapping madly like a grocery sack on a barbed wire fence. All Lester could see was the harum-scarum hurly-burly of a rising storm. Despite everything, he didn't realize that the disturbance was coming from Fish and that, behind Fish, I didn't have a single hair out of place or a single rustle in my skirt; it was as though I were standing in the still, calm eye of a cyclone.

But Bobbi and Will Junior saw it all, and now they understood perfectly. Now they knew, sure as sure as sure.

Bobbi and Will no longer had any doubts whatsoever that the Beaumont kids were different. That the Beaumont kids were extraordinarily, freakishly not normal. But all told, when it came right down to it, Bobbi and Will realized that we were also pretty amazing.

Chapter 21

"SCUMBLING A SAVVY IS LIKE SPREADING a thin layer of paint over yourself," Momma had told Fish and Rocket when she'd had them painting pictures with her on a winter morning before the holidays. I'd stayed home sick from school that day and was enjoying lying on the sofa watching my brothers render stormy ocean waves from memory. My ears had perked up when Momma started talking about how to scumble, and I paid close attention to her words.

"If you don't use enough paint," Momma continued, "your savvy will come through too strong, causing some pretty big problems for both you and the rest of the world." Momma laughed as Fish and Rocket both made faces—they already knew far too well about such troubles.

Momma went on, "If you use too much paint, you'll not only obscure your savvy completely, but most everything else in life will become dull and uninteresting for you too. You can't get rid of part of what makes you *you* and be happy."

Momma took her paintbrush and dipped it into a color much lighter than that already on her canvas. She brushed the light paint over the dark, completely covering it. But the light paint didn't block out the dark paint all the way. Instead, that pale color had a softening, blending effect, making the darker shade harmonize with the rest of the painting.

"So a well-scumbled savvy gives you clarity and control," lectured Momma. "You have to let your own know-how, your own unique color, shine through as a something-special others can't quite put a finger on."

Momma had made it sound so easy. But managing

that kind of success with a savvy could be more of a high-wire act than a cakewalk. Depending on the person and the savvy, it could take years to gain enough control to mingle easily with the rest of the world, and even adulthood didn't offer any guarantees of an effortless fit. That's why, back in Kansaska-Nebransas, homeschooling went way, way beyond reading, writing, and arithmetic.

Fish's wind blew stronger and stronger through the dark alleyway. I wasn't sure he'd stormed that mightily since the day his hurricane had sent us packing. After turning thirteen, Fish had never stopped needing to work extra hard to let his own particular color shine through all his dark storm clouds. Having a really powerful savvy like his was similar to waking up with a savage temper: It required a lot of extra effort and patience to control.

There in Emerald, far from home, with Fish storming his storm and The Great and Powerful Ozzie knocked down to size inside the diner, I was starting to feel low on heart, and my brains and bravery weren't so sure either. Fish and I weren't in Kansaska-Nebransas anymore and we didn't have any yellow bricks to guide us, just a big pink bus and the yellow stripe-stripe-stripes on the highway.

I let out a shriek as a four-cornered No Parking Any Time sign ripped from its post and spun through the air in the spiraling wind.

The sign flew toward Bobbi and Will as I screamed, "Watch out!"

Fish caught sight of the plummeting sign and spun on his heel. In a wink and a blink he turned aside the hurtling object with a controlled burst of deflecting wind.

Controlled. Fish had controlled his outburst—aimed it even. The sign clattered to the ground from its midair path, like a kite plummeting to the earth when the wind suddenly dies. Fish took a step back in surprise and his storm shut down faster than it had started. My brother looked at his hands. He appeared to have finally found the right color paint to complement his savvy.

"Cool," he said under his breath. Fish then turned toward a sagging cardboard box that had come to rest about ten feet away. Looking at the box, he squinted his eyes, making his eyebrows come together above his nose with the intensity of his concentration. After a second, the box lifted slightly, and then tumbled away down the alley, carried on a focused gust of air. Fish smiled, then turned back to Bobbi and Will, concern rearranging his features, his fury gone with the wind.

"You two okay?" he asked, taking a hesitant step toward them. For once, Bobbi was speechless; not even her little angel had much to say. Bobbi nodded, looking dazed. Behind her, Will Junior was grinning at us like he was finally sure he understood the joke.

"Excellent," pronounced Will with a satisfied laugh.

Lester Swan was still hanging out the door of the bus, looking up at the rising moon and the clear, tranquil sky. "Twister country," he muttered, oblivious to the true nature of the haywire weather. "Come on, kids. Everybody in. It's time for us to move on."

Climbing back onto the bus, Will sat down next to me, still smiling, his left knee bumping my right one. To my surprise, and everyone else's too, Bobbi sat down by Fish. Will picked gravel from the fries in his burger basket before offering it around to the group. Aside from Samson, who sat happily digging his finger into the center of the stolen pie now resting on Lill's knees, Will had the only remaining dinner, the other baskets littering the ground between the diner and the bus.

"I think we ought to put a bit of distance between ourselves and Emerald, Lester," Lill suggested, looking anxiously out the window. Lester nodded his head and started the engine; he seemed worn out by his uncharacteristic exploits and glad to have someone else tell him what to do.

"Where should I take you, Lill?" he said over his shoulder as he pulled the bus out of the alley behind the diner.

"Well, I don't think I want to go back home just yet,"

Lill replied. "Ozzie knows where I live, and after the way we left him . . ." She trailed off with a shiver, then continued, "You were on your way to Salina with these kids, Lester. Maybe we should just head down there. That is, if y'all don't mind me tagging along?"

Lill looked around to each of us. We all shook our heads and bit our tongues. It wasn't like any of us would tell her no. We hadn't even asked permission to be on that bus ourselves.

"Lester?"

Lester hardly had to answer the big woman. He was so glad Lill wanted to travel on with us that he had tears in his eyes.

"I'd take you anywhere, Lill Kiteley," he said.

My heart leaped at the thought of getting to Salina, and of seeing Poppa at last. I knew, after the report on the TV in the diner, what Rocket's electrical damage might mean for Poppa—my brother had to be fearfully upset to cause such monstrous mayhem. Even if I couldn't do anything to help Poppa after all, I needed to hold his hand and kiss his cheek and let him know that I was there and that he was loved.

As he drove, Lester's shoulders began to convulse more violently than ever and the thin man started squirming in his seat like a small child.

"What is it, Lester?" asked Lill, seeing his discomfort. Lester cast a glance over his shoulder at us kids.

"Well," he said, all milk-toast and mouse-like, "I've got a delivery to make in Wymore in the morning and my b-boss won't be too pleased if I miss it. I've already gummed up the rest of my deliveries today, if I b-bungle another . . . well, I might lose my job," he sniffed. "I might lose my bus."

"Oh poor Lester," Carlene sniggered. *"Poor, stupid Lester. What would he do without his precious bus?"*

"He'd sell coffee at the bus station, that's what," clucked Rhonda.

"But—!" we all began to protest.

"We have to get down to Salina Hope, Mr. Swan! We

just have to!" I pleaded. But Lester had set his mind and refused to even look in our direction.

"I can't lose my b-bus," was all he'd say, quiet but firm, as though all his gears had locked into place.

Lill looked perplexed.

"It *would* be a shame for *you* to lose your job too," Lill said with a sigh, looking down sadly at her green waitressing uniform. "But the kidlings, Lester? What about them? What about Salina and their father? Surely there are some folks down there waiting for these kids?"

To this, nobody replied. Lester twitched. The rest of us worried and fidgeted. Lill's eyes narrowed as she looked around at us all inside the dim interior of the bus. Bobbi busied herself with unrolling her last bit of Bubble Tape. Fish whistled noiselessly. Will Junior just stared at his knees, running a hand through his curly hair, and I tugged at a loose piece of white rickrack that hung down from the sleeve of my dress. Only Samson managed not to look noticeably guilty, as he sat next to

Lill, alternating bites of hamburger with snitches of pie.

Lill stiffened and crossed her arms over her chest. "All right, what's going on here? I may have a knack for being tardy, but I'm not usually so late to catch on. I think maybe someone ought to start explaining to me exactly what I've got myself into the middle of. Right now."

Chapter 22

IT WAS WITH MORE THAN A little chagrin that we told Lill what we'd done. Wanting to leave Emerald behind, Lester headed east through the dark as we took turns telling Lill how we'd snuck aboard Lester's bus believing he would be returning to Salina. We told her how Lester had turned left instead of right, north instead of south, and how we'd found ourselves heading away from Salina and the hospital and our poppa.

Lill's face did not change throughout the telling or for several minutes after, when an awkward silence fell throughout the bus. The only sounds came from the knocks and pings of the engine and from the voices in my head.

"We're dead, we're dead," Bobbi's tattoo repeated over and over like a nervous heartbeat.

Lill sat still for a long, long time. Samson had finished his burger, and had carved a substantial crater in the pie, and now he reached out to sneak fries from Will's basket. The rest of us hadn't touched its contents. We'd all lost our appetites.

Finally the big woman let out a long, slow sigh with a sound like an angel falling down from one cloud to another.

"I sure know how to find my way into trouble," Lill said, more to herself than to any one of us. "Today I've lost both my car and my job. And now it looks like I've gone and lost my senses too."

We continued to watch Lill, cautiously hopeful that she wasn't going to turn us in.

"Listen here, all of you." Lill raised her little voice over the noisy engine. "I'm going to tell you what we're going to do." Lester smiled. He seemed to dote on women who told him what to do, but at least Lill wasn't anything like Carlene or Rhonda. Lill lay down the law. The plan was to continue east toward Lincoln to find a motel, giving us some distance from Emerald but getting us off the road sooner rather than later. Lill didn't like the thought of us being out on the highways at night and she wanted us kids to call our parents to let them know we were safe and sound and headed for Salina in the morning. I could tell Lill was struggling with knowing the right thing to do, unsure how much messier one day could get.

I contemplated that for a while myself. The last thing I wanted was to get Lester and Lill into any hot water just because I'd had the stupid idea that I could find my own way down to Salina. I knew that it was my job to look after the grown-ups now. It was my job to keep them safe and out of trouble, and I supposed if that meant waiting until morning to get to Poppa, that would just have to be the way things were going to be, even if it felt almost too much to bear.

In the short hours since we'd climbed aboard that

bus, we'd become an odd band of renegades. We kids promised Lill that we would call home as soon as we reached the motel, but I kept my fingers crossed behind my back. Lester was clearly relieved to have someone else making the decisions; it seemed he'd used up every last drop of his tiny reservoir of nerve to keep the bus on its original course for his deliveries.

Lill didn't say anything more about losing her job and no one brought it up. She counted out the cash that The Great and Powerful Ozzie had paid her, squinting at it in the dim light inside the bus.

"Well, kidlings," she announced halfheartedly, "I believe that I've got more than enough here to pay for a couple of rooms at a motel. Can you find us someplace out of the way, Lester?"

"Anything you say, Lill."

I watched Lill gaze fondly at Lester. I could tell by the way she looked at him that she found something in the man she admired. Maybe it had been the way Lester stopped to rescue her from her broken-down car, or how he'd helped her pick her money up off the floor, or his spur-of-the-moment plunder of the pie from the diner. Lester might not have looked the part of a hero, but I suppose you never can tell right off who might have a piece of Prince Charming deep down inside.

Lester drove on for some time before finding us just the right motel. The Lincoln Sleepy 10 had only a few cars in the parking lot, and its vacancy sign was buzzing and blinking like a bug light.

The Sleepy 10 was located on the far side of the city, across from a Mega Mega Mart and a row of loud red and yellow fast-food restaurants. We all stayed on the bus, which Lester parked well away from the motel, while the deliveryman did the checking in using Lill's cash. After seeing my face on the TV at the Emerald Truck Stop Diner, I was none too keen on waltzing around in public any more than I had to, so I was glad to wait on the bus with the others.

Lill told Lester to get two rooms, though Lester insisted he'd be sleeping on his bus to "p-protect his inventory." I hoped the motel would come complete with thin white soaps wrapped up in paper, little bottles of shampoo, and crisp white towels folded up snug in the bathroom, all of which would make me right pleased.

"You're all up on the second floor," said Lester when he handed Lill the room keys and watched us climb down out of the bus. He was just as tense and jumpy as ever, and he looked almost sad as we left him there. For a second I wondered if Lester might panic and leave us there in the middle of the night; I supposed even less humble heroes might've thought about it. But the way Lester looked at Lill made me doubt it.

"Promise you'll be here in the morning, Mr. Swan?" I called back to him before he closed the door of the bus. Lester tilted his head like a listening dog, and gave me a funny look.

"Where would I go?" he asked. And that was all the answer I needed.

Lill ushered us toward stairs that led to our rooms. Fish sniffed the air as we passed a locked door with a single window down on the first level. The sign next to the door said *Pool—Guests Only.*

"Water," Fish said simply.

The pool sat, still and empty, reflecting dancing green light across the walls and ceiling of the small room. At any other time, being so close to that much water would've made Fish nervous and fidgety, but when I glanced his way he looked calm as calm.

Lill didn't miss the way we all looked at that pool through the window, but she ordered us up the stairs ahead of her with the command of a drill sergeant in green and white camouflage. When we reached the second floor, Lill took the lead, holding Samson's hand while looking for our rooms and fumbling one-handed with the room keys.

The rest of us dropped behind.

"We can't call home," I whispered to Will. He looked from Lill back to me, his eyes questioning. Lill was farther ahead of us now, moving up the long hallway. I reached forward and tugged on the back of Bobbi's shirt, noticing the way the angel tattoo on her back now reclined on one elbow, wings folded in, picking its teeth with the end of its pointed tail indifferently.

"Bobbi, we can't call home," I said to her.

"Duh," she replied and rolled her eyes at me.

"Of course she knows that," said the angel. But I ignored it.

"Fish?"

"I know, I know," he whispered back at me. "We can't call home. But just how do you think we'll get away with *that?*"

"I've got a plan," I said.

"Oh goodie," said Bobbi. "She's got a plan."

THE TRICK WOULD BE IN THE timing. Wrangling Lester earlier in the day had been surprisingly easy, but I knew flimflamming Lill was going to be a lot harder—she had to believe, without a doubt, that we'd called home or she wouldn't be satisfied.

I remembered Bobbi mimicking her mother over meat loaf at the dinner table the night before and how she'd sounded just like Miss Rosemary. I also remembered how Will Junior had threatened Bobbi with telling their parents how she called in to school, using her mother's voice, to excuse her own absences when she ditched classes.

With two motel rooms, one across the hall from the other, I figured we just might be able to pull off my scheme.

It was for Lill's own good, I told myself again and again. I had to keep her and Lester out of trouble. If we called home now, who knew what might happen? But if we could lay low until we reached Salina Hope Hospital tomorrow, maybe Lester and Lill could get on their way without anyone knowing that they'd helped us out, or blaming them wrongly for carrying us off.

Lill inspected both rooms before assigning the boys to one and us girls to the other. Bobbi and I were in 214 with Lill, and the three boys were in 215.

"Just pick up your phone when it rings, Fish," I whispered to my brother before we separated. "Pick it up, but don't say anything. Stay on the phone and let Bobbi in if she knocks. We've got to rely on Bobbi now." Fish nodded, glancing at Bobbi dubiously, and then followed Samson and Will Junior into Room 215.

Once inside the room across the hall, Lill pointed to

the telephone and said, "Bobbi, please call your parents now and tell them where you all are. They must be worried sick, the poor folks."

Bobbi shot me a wide-eyed What-Do-I-Do-Now? look, and moved slowly toward the phone. She picked up the receiver like she was moving through water, watching Lill as the woman removed her sweater and hung it on the doorknob of the closet. I nearly jumped for joy when Lill flicked the light on in the bathroom and closed the door behind her.

Bobbi may not have had a savvy in the same way as we Beaumonts, but it was time for her to use her very own special kind of know-how. Before Lill could return, I rushed to Bobbi's side and told her exactly what she had to do. She looked at me like I'd lost my marbles.

"She thinks you're crazy," her angel tattoo sang in my head.

"This isn't like calling in to trick the school secretary, Mibs," Bobbi whispered harshly. "What if it doesn't work?"

But we could already hear Lill washing her hands in the bathroom and had no time to argue. "Just do it," I said, pointing to the number printed on the motel phone.

Bobbi dialed, glancing over her shoulder toward the bathroom as she made a room-to-room call. Lill opened the door and stepped back out into the room, smoothing her skirt and scraping at the pie spatter that had dried on the front of it. She looked up as Bobbi started talking.

"Hi Mom, it's Bobbi." Bobbi shot me a glare as she pretended to talk to her mother, with Fish now sitting silently on the other end of the line across the hall. But Bobbi was a good actress; at times during her brief, one-sided conversation, even I forgot that she was faking, as she explained to dead air where we were and how we'd gotten there and how we would get down to the hospital in Salina tomorrow.

"No Mother, we're perfectly safe. I promise!" Bobbi insisted. "Yes Mother, you can talk to Mibs. She's right here . . ."

Bobbi rolled her eyes and slumped her shoulders dramatically as she held the telephone out to me. I looked sheepishly at Lill and took the phone, hoping I could do half as well at playacting as Bobbi had. I held the receiver to my chest for a moment, as though looking for the courage to put it to my ear.

"I'm going to check on the boys," Bobbi said, grabbing a room key and getting up to leave the room. "My mother wants to talk to you next, Lill," she said, opening the door, then letting it slam shut behind her. Lill's face was pale. She chewed the cuticle on her pinkie and took a deep breath. I could tell she wasn't looking forward to the idea of talking to the preacher's wife, and I felt shamed and sorry for tricking her. *It's for her own good,* I reminded myself, then I lifted the phone to my ear just as I heard Bobbi knocking on the door across the hall.

"Miss Rosemary? It's Mibs. I'm sorry . . ." I started out. I measured my pauses as I spoke haltingly into the phone, trying to make it seem as though I was getting a tongue-lashing.

There was a clatter on the other end of the line.

"You're going straight to hell, Mississippi Beaumont," said Bobbi in a voice so much like Miss Rosemary's that I nearly dropped the phone. Then she snickered. "Put that waitress on. Then start praying." Bobbi was way too good at this. I hoped she'd go easy on poor Lill.

I held the telephone out to Lill and swallowed hard.

"She wants to talk to you," I said.

I held my breath the entire time Lill was on the phone with Bobbi-slash-Miss Rosemary. I wasn't entirely sure what Bobbi said—I was only able to catch a word or two of Bobbi's end of the conversation when her voice rose in pitch and volume and carried out from the receiver. But Lill worked hard to make it known that all us kids were healthy and whole and in good hands with her and Lester. She gave over the name of our motel and the phone number.

"We'd be glad to bring the kidlings home, or down to the hospital in Salina, Mrs. Meeks, unless you'd rather come and get them right away," Lill said nervously.

My lungs felt fit to burst. I wished I could hear Bobbi's reply; that girl was fast on her feet when it came to deceit, and I couldn't decide whether I admired her or felt sorry for her for having such a skill.

At last the conversation began to wind down. "That will be just fine, ma'am," said Lill. "We'll see you all in Salina tomorrow then.

"Yes, ma'am . . .

"Thank you, ma'am . . .

"God bless you too, ma'am."

I could just picture Bobbi in the room across the hall, saying "God bless you" to Lill in Miss Rosemary's stern voice. I shook my head, praying Bobbi didn't push her luck and wishing she'd just hang up the phone already.

When Lill finally set the telephone down, color was returning to her cheeks.

"That went better than I expected," said Lill with her little smile. "That Rosemary seems like a good, strong woman. She's going to call your family and tell them you and your brothers are safe, Mibs."

"Great," I said halfheartedly, feeling low, low, low about our double-dealing deception.

I heard the key swipe the lock and the door opened. Bobbi, Will, and Fish all sauntered into the room, looking like a bunch of cats who'd just finished feasting on an entire flock of canaries. Fortunately, Lill was so relieved to be off the phone, she didn't even notice.

"IF I'M GOING TO BE RESPONSIBLE for you kidlings until tomorrow, I'd better get us some supplies." Lill was so happy to believe that things were sorted out and settled with the adults, she looked five years younger and three inches taller. "Would anybody like to cross the road with me? I saw a Mega Mega Mart as we drove in and I have a bit of money left."

We all shook our heads, saying nothing. Better to lay low, I thought. After all, people were still looking for us.

"Nobody?" said Lill in her little voice. "Well, all right then. Why don't y'all sit tight and watch some TV until

I get back." Lill moved to pick up the remote control from the desk by the telephone, but Fish jumped up and grabbed it before she could reach it. Why is it that adults are always telling kids to go watch television as though we have nothing better to do?

"I got it," said Fish, holding up the remote and smiling a cockeyed Fish smile. Lill looked around at the four of us, now spread out across the beds and chairs in the room.

"Where's—?"

"Samson's okay," said Fish, anticipating her question. "He's in the other room. We're all okay. You can go shop—we'll be fine." Another smile.

"Well, okay," said Lill, a bit unsure. She cast one look back at us before leaving the room, as though something suspicious still tickled her senses. "I'll be back in a shake—no later than twenty or thirty minutes."

As soon as Lill stepped out, the four of us all gulped for air as though we'd not drawn breath since getting to the motel.

"I can't believe that worked," said Bobbi.

"Remind me to *never* tell Mother that you can do that," said Will.

"We've got a bigger problem," said Fish, ruining our small moment of triumph by turning on the television and flipping to a local news channel. It took less than a minute before our pictures flashed across the screen with ALERT! MISSING! ALERT! scrolling along the bottom, just as Fish and I had seen on the little TV back in Emerald.

"You've *got* to be kidding me!" moaned Bobbi, who, like Will, hadn't seen the newscast at the diner.

Will stared slack-jawed at the screen with his sister. Looking resigned and unhappy, Fish tossed the television remote back and forth from hand to hand like it was a hot potato.

"Man, are we in trouble," said Will, shaking his head with a grimace as his own image flashed up on the screen. "Maybe we really *should* have called home."

"It's better that we didn't," said Bobbi. "Do you really want state troopers storming in here tonight?

You know that if we'd called home, Mother would have phoned big brother and he'd have been here in no time flat—he and every other trooper from here to Topeka. What do you think would happen to Lester and Lill then? They'd get in huge trouble."

Will turned his head sharp and sudden.

"Bill's more than a little protective," Bobbi continued.

"He's going to be mad," said Will, and for the first time on that whole trip Will looked painfully, miserably unhappy.

"Shh!" Fish shushed everyone with a violent and well-aimed blast of wind, looking momentarily pleased with himself. Then he turned up the volume of the television.

". . . according to a source close to the family, the father of three of the missing children is one of the victims of last Thursday's ten-car pile up on Highway 81 outside Salina, Kansas. The man sustained serious injuries and is still unconscious and in critical condition at Salina Hope Hospital."

I threw myself back onto the floral bedspread and put my hands over my face.

"It will be all right," the singsong voice said inside my head.

I looked up at Bobbi, who was looking right back at me intently. She nodded at me once.

"It will be all right," the angel's voice repeated. Bobbi gave me a brief, kindly smile—it was there and gone again like a flash of Rocket's sparks.

The older girl got up and turned off the TV. "That stays off," she said, looking from me to Will to Fish. We all nodded and watched as Bobbi unplugged the cord from the wall for good measure.

"It will be all right," Bobbi said out loud to everyone.

Lill returned nearly an hour later with a smile almost big enough for her body and several bags from the Mega Mega Mart. She dumped their contents onto the closest bed.

"Today's your lucky day, kidlings," she said as we

checked out the pile, amazed by how much stuff she'd come back with. There was a mountain of candy bars, T-shirts, chips, lip gloss in both pink and red, Pop-Tarts, playing cards, magazines, Q-tips, nail polish, crayons, duct tape, a new first aid kit, a clean new necktie for Lester, a Slinky, seven toothbrushes, six feet of Snappy Strawberry Bubble Tape for Bobbi, five pairs of flip-flops, four sticks of deodorant, a package of combs, animal crackers, underwear, and swimsuits.

Lill laughed. "I just kept on shopping until I was sure I'd spent every dollar Ozzie made me pick up off the floor. That money was too greasy to get attached to, just like that diner." She tossed Fish a pair of swim trunks. "I had to guess on all the sizes, so the fit may not be perfect."

"We can go swimming?" I asked, holding up a purple suit with yellow straps that looked almost right for me.

"Kids and pools . . . well, they're like birds and sky, aren't they?" said Lill. "Besides, even bad kids need to have a little fun sometimes."

We all stared at Lill, dumbfounded.

"Well, go on," she laughed again, "stop staring at me like I just dropped out of the heavens and get changed. What good is a pool without any kids in it? I'm going out to the bus to check on Lester; I've got some ideas for him about how to deliver all those pink Bibles. I think he just needs to take a different approach. Lester just needs some confidence in his own skills." She waved the duct tape in the air. "He also needs some help covering up all those broken windows in that bus of his."

Lill put the roll of tape around her wrist like a big silver bracelet and picked up the new necktie—not pink, but blue with green stripes. She smoothed the silky tie with her fingers, smiling to herself; Lester wasn't the only one working on his charms. Maybe some good would come from this big mess I'd made after all.

THE BOYS RETURNED TO THEIR ROOM across the hall to change into the colorful swim trunks Lill had picked out for them. Bobbi went into the bathroom, happily toting a cherry red bikini. I changed as quick as I could into the purple one-piece, frustrated that it fit too loosely despite all manner of yellow straps and strings that I did my best to make heads and tails of.

I'd never felt bashful in a swimsuit before that day, but things in my life were changing faster than I could keep up with; I felt a tad vulnerable being a jig shy of jaybird-naked in a suit that better suited someone older. I pulled an oversized T-shirt over my head just as Bobbi emerged looking trim and pretty and all grown-up and filled-in in her bikini. She wrinkled her nose when she looked at me.

"What's with the T-shirt?"

"My suit doesn't fit so good."

"Let me see."

I removed the shirt and let Bobbi adjust all the yellow straps. By the time she was finished, the swimsuit fit much better.

"Thanks," I said weakly, still shy about leaving the T-shirt behind.

Bobbi shrugged. "No problem." We left the room, making sure no one saw us coming or going, and joined the boys downstairs by the pool.

The room was hot and humid, lined in lime green tile and dusty, artificial plants and trees. The pool was small and shaped like a jelly bean, but just the right size for four kids. Samson was nowhere to be seen, but that didn't worry any of us; everyone was used to his disappearances by now.

Will was already in the pool, his hair wet and dripping into his black eye. Fish stood at the edge of the pool with his arms folded, staring at the water with a determined look hardening his scratched face.

"You getting in?" I asked my brother carefully, keeping my eye on Bobbi's angel, where it shivered on her back, gripping its pointed devil's tail in one hand and reaching up to grasp its halo with the other, as Bobbi stepped down into the water in front of me. Fish smiled his cocky brother smile and nodded.

"I'm good," he said simply.

"Good."

"Cold . . . C-cooold." The water engulfed the picture of the little angel as Bobbi plunged and the faltering voice in my head grew muffled and bleary.

Will Junior vaulted up out of the water and grasped my wrist, pulling me over into the pool next to him with a splash. Getting my head back above the surface and my wet hair out of my eyes, I found Will's face close to mine, his hand still holding my wrist loosely underwater. Then he moved forward and his lips touched mine, quick and awkward with the taste of chlorine and salt, like maybe he'd just slipped and bumped his face into mine accidentally. It happened so fast that I hardly had time to react before a dancing funnel of water splashed Will ferociously in the side of the head.

Will let go of my wrist, coughing and sputtering, trying to recover from the water that had gushed up his nose. Then he looked up at Fish, who was still standing dry as dry next to the pool, his arms folded across his chest and a smug and swaggering smirk inscribed across his face.

"There'll be none of that business with *my* sister," said Fish.

At first I thought Will was going to get angry, and I readied myself for another brawl. Instead Will flashed me an outlaw's smile, then made a sudden move toward Fish, pushing hard at the water in front of him with the palms of his hands, and splashing a sheet of water up at my brother.

"Just *tell* me," Will demanded. "How do you *do* that?"

Fish, taking a deep, deep breath like he was setting aside an entire year's worth of dread, jumped into the water with a big, splashy cannonball and the boys launched into a friendly yet frighteningly powerful water fight; Fish definitely had the upper hand. Still feeling dazed by Will's quick, salty-sweet kiss, I hovered in the water, holding on to the cement lip of the pool, watching the water around me surge and swell as waves splashed over the two boys and sprayed up over the side. The artificial plants lining the room rustled their dusty leaves in the drafts, and fake ficus trees and parlor palms tipped over in their wicker baskets onto the wet floor. But Fish kept things fairly well under control and caused no permanent damage.

I imagined how proud Momma and Poppa and Grandpa Bomba would all be when they found out that Fish had wrestled his savvy and finally come out on top, and I wondered if Fish would be able to go back to school in Hebron now if he wanted to—wouldn't Rocket be wound up and wicked jealous? We'd probably lose power to the house for a week while Rocket sulked.

As the water fight intensified, Bobbi pulled me into the calmer water at the shallow end of the pool and she and I sat on the steps, half in and half out of the water, keeping an eye on the door and watching our brothers nearly drown each other over and over. The sound of Bobbi's angel in my head had grown steadily more muffled and choppy, becoming quieter and quieter in the noisy, echoing pool room. Every now and then, Will Junior would send another smile my way, but I wasn't sure if I wanted to smile back or sink down under the water.

"Will likes you a lot," Bobbi said, still watching the boys. "I think he's liked you since the very first day you started coming to our church." Despite the fact that I was already wise to this tittle-tattle tidbit, my face went pink and hot; having Bobbi say it out loud made me feel awkward, made me feel too young and too old at the same time.

I remembered Poppa giving me my special-occasion dress, just days ago.

"I just thought my little girl deserved something pretty and new to wear for her special birthday," he'd said. Poppa always, *always* called me his little girl. But I wasn't such a little girl anymore. I knew that now, sure as sure.

"So, do you like Will back?" Bobbi wanted to know.

My insides went wishy-washy and I felt my blush turn from pink to red. "I don't know," I said with a shrug that left my shoulders sitting two inches higher than they were before, my head tucked in like Samson's not-dead turtle. "Maybe."

Bobbi looked at me and, to my surprise, she smiled. It was not the snarky smile she normally wore, or the quick flash of a secret smile she'd let slip back up in the motel room. No, this particular smile was the glad, lingering kind that one friend gives another when they need it most.

"That's okay," Bobbi said. "Don't sweat it. *Believe* me, take your time." That sounded funny coming from Bobbi, who, for all of her sixteen years, seemed more than ready to speed right along. As if to highlight this even more, Bobbi let out a short, wistful sigh, flicking at the surface of the water with one finger. "It's too bad Rocket's not here. Every time he comes to church, the room feels all tingly. I bet *he'd* be fun to kiss."

I looked at Bobbi's pierced eyebrow and her cherry red bikini, and I tried to imagine her kissing my brother, sparks and all.

"Why are *you* in such a hurry?" I asked her.

Bobbi snorted. "You can read minds. You tell me."

I concentrated on Bobbi and tried to listen. I tried to hear what she was thinking, tried to hear the voice of her angel tattoo inside my head, but it was silent . . . gone. All I could hear was the raucous splish-splash of the water and the echoes of the boys' laughter bouncing off the walls.

"I can't," I said after a moment. "I—I don't know

why." Then I remembered the very first thing that musical voice had ever said to me. It had been only hours ago, back in the church kitchen in Hebron, though it felt like a lifetime had passed since then.

She's really very lonely, you know . . .

"Is it hard to be the preacher's daughter?" I asked after some considering.

Bobbi looked at me sharply. "What do you mean?"

"I just imagine that people probably expect you to be perfect as perfect all the time, even though you probably just want to be able to mess up like everyone else," I said, thinking of Momma and her savvy. "I expect it could get awfully lonesome sometimes." Bobbi didn't say anything, so I continued on with a little more backbone, lowering my shoulders an inch and sticking my head out of my shell. "Maybe that's what makes you want to move on fast and push other people off. Maybe you don't want to have to set the preacher-perfect example."

"I thought you just said you couldn't read my mind right now," said Bobbi, pulling her knees up to her chest on the step of the pool and wrapping her arms around them tightly.

"Well, I'm just guessing. Your little angel's not talking much at the moment. Maybe it's the water."

"Angel?" Bobbi looked at me inquiringly.

"Your tattoo," I said. "The tattoo of the angel with the devil's tail. The one you've got on your back. That's how I hear things—there has to be ink."

"You mean you can read my mind because I stuck on a temporary tattoo this morning?"

"Temporary?" I repeated.

"Well . . . *yeah*. Did you think it was real?" Bobbi stood up and twisted around, trying unsuccessfully to see the tattoo. When I looked, I was surprised to find only a few specks of color freckling her skin where the angel had been, the rest of the image now completely washed off by the water and chemicals in the pool. For a moment I was almost sad as I realized that the angel's short-lived voice was gone for good. But mostly I was relieved. Relieved that now I could learn about Bobbi the normal way, or not at all, if that's what we chose.

Sitting back down next to me on the steps in the water, Bobbi sighed. "Mibs, do you ever feel like your life is just some weird dream and someday you'll wake up and find that you're someone else entirely?" Bobbi slipped down one step until the water of the pool came up over her mouth, nearly to her nose. She blew soft bubbles of air out in front of her and closed her eyes. We both bobbed and swayed in the water, churned up as it was by the boys' aquatic battle.

I thought about her question for a long time. I could feel my hair starting to dry and the tips of my fingers and toes begin to pucker and wrinkle. If someone had said those same words to me yesterday I might have shrugged them off. But a lot can change in a day.

A lot.

Chapter 26

WHEN WE GOT BACK UPSTAIRS, WE found Samson curled up snug as a bug under the table in the boys' room, sound asleep and clutching the Slinky from the Mega Mega Mart to his face in a way that was sure to leave a funny mark in the morning. He'd pulled off one of the flowery motel bedspreads and draped it over the table like a tent, leaving the beds for Will and Fish, but he'd taken all the pillows with him. In the girls' room, Bobbi took one bed for her whole self and I shared the other with Lill and her big angel feet and her lumberjack snore.

Just before she fell asleep, Lill sighed. "You never can tell when a bad thing might make a good thing happen," she said quietly, and at first I wasn't sure if she was talking to herself or to me.

It wasn't easy for me to fall asleep that night. The mattress was hard and the bedsheets were rough against my cheek. Lill's words haunted me, keeping my mind running like a mouse on a wheel. I thought about the boys across the hall, and about Will kissing me in the pool. I thought about Lester on his cot outside in the bus, and Lill next to me dreaming of him. I thought about Bobbi and how she was beginning to feel like something awfully close to a friend. And then I thought about the homeless man behind the diner and about Poppa tucked in his bed at Salina Hope—and I wondered if either of them would ever be able to find any good in all the bad they were caught in.

Before Poppa's accident the biggest bad in my life had been Grandma Dollop dying. I remembered standing next to Poppa at Grandma's funeral when I was ten years old. He'd held my hand the entire time. There in the cemetery, Grandma had been laid to rest surrounded by flowers and family. Jars and jars of her radio favorites were stacked on and around and even inside the casket like Grandma Dollop was one of the pharaohs of Egypt taking all of her treasures with her.

Aunt Dinah and Uncle Autry were there with their families, as well as a few of the remaining great-aunts and -uncles and second cousins who were able to make the journey south. Even Grandma's light-fingered sister, Jubilee, was there, though Momma had been sure to hide all of her jewelry and kept a close watch on the silverware when Jubilee came over to the house for the wake.

Grandma's was a funeral like no other. Momma and Aunt Dinah had sat like sturdy bookends on either side of Grandpa Bomba, with their arms linked tightly through his, supporting him as the preacher said his words and prayers.

But when that preacher reached his last *Amen,* sorrow and grief unleashed the savvy of young and old alike. Lightning struck a nearby tree. A swarm of dragonflies and bumblebees filled the air above the casket, dancing and darting like an array of living fireworks. The grass beneath our feet grew thick and tall and the flowers in bud opened up to bloom, filling the air with a heady fragrance. The underground sprinklers came on like fountains, surrounding us all in a grand display of seemingly choreographed plumes and jets of waltzing water, yet not a single drop fell down upon the mourners.

And finally, as the tears rolled down Grandpa Bomba's cheeks, the ground began to rumble. Headstones rocked and the folding chairs shuddered and rattled to and fro with all the folks still sitting in them holding tight. The earth shook violently and Grandma's glass jars began to topple and break, filling the air with a riot of sound. Organ music and gospel choirs, country-western ballads and oom-pah-pah polka music flew into the air like boisterous confetti. Great voices lit upon the breeze with words that were both sweet and sharp, speeches that were moving and powerful. There were words like *dream* and words like *freedom* that lingered in the air in the voices of women, men, and children.

And Poppa had wrapped his arms around me then, and we'd closed our eyes, listening together to the spectacle of sounds, to the procession of melodies, to the vanishing radio waves of Grandma Dollop's savvy.

These memories, and more, flooded my mind as I tossed and turned in that motel bed outside Lincoln. All my running away and all of this fuss and trouble was for Poppa, I reminded myself. It was all for Poppa.

But something about that idea nagged at me—something flummoxed me deep, deep, deep in the pit of my stomach with a kink and a snarl.

I *had* run away for Poppa . . . hadn't I?

I'd fled the church in Hebron, convinced that I had to—convinced that I could wake up my poppa and make things right. But now, lying in the too dark room of the Lincoln Sleepy 10 in a Mega Mega Mart T-shirt with the tag still attached and scritch-scratching my neck, it occurred to me that maybe Poppa hadn't been the only reason I'd run away. Running away meant running *from* something. When I walked out of that church in Hebron, I was running toward Poppa, but maybe—*maybe*—I was running *away* from something else. Running away from my unexpected, unwished-for savvy. Running away from the fact that I was growing up and life was changing as quick and sure and electrifying and terrifying as Rocket's sparks or Fish's hurricane or even a very first kiss. These thoughts kept me wide-awake late into the night.

The boys moseyed into our room just after nine o'clock the next morning, balancing Styrofoam plates of thick, crisp waffles and plastic cups of orange juice from the breakfast bar downstairs. Will Junior wore a long black Mega Mega Mart T-shirt and his hair was tousled and tangled. Since running away from Hebron, Will had almost completely lost the serious, serious look that I was so used to seeing him wear.

"It's getting late," said Lill, opening the curtains and

nearly blinding me with morning sunlight. "I let you sleep too long."

"Wake up, Sleeping Beauty," Will said, shoving a plate of sticky, syrupy waffles my way.

"You went downstairs?" I said in a whisper, making sure Lill couldn't hear. "Did anyone see you?"

Will leaned in close to my ear. "No one saw us, Mibs," he whispered back before sitting down on the edge of the other bed next to Fish, who had already dug into his breakfast.

Bobbi was in the bathroom, taking forever to get herself ready, and Lill fussed and mussed over Samson, trying to run a comb through his mane of dark hair before he could escape into the recesses of the empty motel closet. Across from me, Fish let go a belch to be proud of and Will Junior matched it in length and volume as though trying to beat a world record.

I wrinkled up my nose at them as I cut my waffles. "I thought you wanted to grow up to be just like your daddy, Will Junior," I scolded, trying not to let on that I was still feeling unsettled by his kiss in the pool. But the boy just smiled at me and winked.

"I do."

Fish snorted and jabbed Will in the ribs with his elbow, dripping syrup on the floor with his fork. "Don't tell me Pastor Meeks can belch like that," he said through a mouthful of waffle.

"Pastor Meeks can't," Will replied with another shameless grin.

Lill chose that moment to try to turn on the television, wanting to check the weather. We all turned to her with a sudden shout of "DON'T!" that nearly made that poor woman sprout wings and fly. Fish stood up so fast he knocked his plate of waffles facedown onto the floor. He bumped Will, who elbowed the plastic cup of orange juice on the nightstand next to him and sent it spilling and dripping into the drawer with the Bible and the phone book and the pizza delivery coupons. Bobbi unlocked the bathroom door and stepped out in time for the rest of us to make a dash for towels and water.

Lester knocked just as things were returning to order. He was wearing the new tie Lill had bought him, along with a clean shirt and a fresh pair of overalls.

"Time to go," he said with a broad smile just for Lill. Lill straightened the knot in Lester's tie, returning his smile and letting one hand linger lightly on the man's chest.

"You look real fine, Lester," said Lill, beaming.

Since everyone else was ready to go, I dressed as quickly as I could in the bathroom. I brushed my teeth and combed my hair. I put on a little shiny red lip gloss that Bobbi had left on the counter, then thought better of it and dabbed it back off again with a tissue. Before leaving the bathroom, I cheerfully added a paper-wrapped soap to the pocket of my dress that still held Will's birthday present pen. Then I joined the others and we all flop-flapped down the hall in our new Mega Mega Mart flip-flops, following Lill and Lester downstairs toward the Heartland Bible Supply bus like a gaggle of flat-footed goslings, keeping a lookout for any unwanted attention.

Ahead of me, Lill laced her large hand through Lester's arm and I tried not to listen to Carlene and Rhonda as they carried on at length about his new crush; though, today their voices didn't seem as loud and nasty as usual.

"I didn't think my boy would ever find himself a decent woman," said Rhonda. *"I suppose he'll mess it up."*

"'Decent woman?' What was I—chopped liver?" sniped Carlene. *"It wasn't my fault Lester couldn't see a good thing when it was right in front of his face."*

"Lester always liked liver," Rhonda snapped back. *"You, Carlene, are just a scrawny old chicken gizzard."*

I thought about those two gals and their constant griping and bellyaching, and my head swam with questions. If I could tell what Lester was thinking or feeling by listening to those voices in my head, why did they always talk about him like he wasn't even there? They were always cutting him down to the quick. It seemed like those two ladies had had such an effect on him that now it was only their voices he heard loud,

loud, loud. Was it their nasty chit-chat that told Lester who he was? No wonder the man had a stutter and a twitch.

Maybe it's like that for everyone, I thought. Maybe we all have other people's voices running higgledy-piggledy through our heads all the time. I thought how often my poppa and momma were there inside my head with me, telling me right from wrong. Or how the voices of Ashley Bing and Emma Flint sometimes got stuck under my skin, taunting me and making me feel low, even when they weren't around. I began to realize how hard it was to separate out all the voices to hear the single, strong one that came just from me.

Climbing back up into the big pink Heartland Bible Supply bus, the morning warm and bright, I tried to listen past Carlene and Rhonda; I tried to hear if there was any of Lester's own voice left in Lester. The more I watched and listened, the more it became clear as clear that whenever Lill smiled Lester's way, or whenever she spoke to him as we traveled down the highway, Carlene and Rhonda seemed to lose their sway. Lill shone on Lester like the sun. And on his arms, his sleeves rolled up, the women's scowling, animated faces dissolved back into the thin black lines of lifeless tattoos.

Maybe Lill *was* an angel, I thought to myself; maybe she was Lester's angel, sent down from heaven to clear the voices from his head.

I turned my eyes away from the adults, choosing a seat by one of the few windows not threaded with cracks or covered in cardboard and silvery duct tape. I watched out the window as we bumped and thumped toward Wymore and Lester's next delivery, passing an endless landscape of grizzled cornfields. The earth was yawning and stretching here, turning green at the toes of the brown and broken stalks of last year's harvest. It was spring and the whole world was coming back to life. The whole world was waking up. Now, I thought to myself, if only Poppa would too.

Chapter 27

WE ARRIVED IN WYMORE JUST AS the morning's second service was ending at the big brick church off Tenth Street. Lester parked the bus in front of the building and waited as Lill straightened his tie one more time and brushed crumbs from his shirt. The man positively beamed at Lill's spit and polish attention, and his shoulders gave neither a hitch nor a twitch.

"Now, don't forget what we talked about," she continued encouragingly. "See if you can deliver those Bibles right to the minister's wife. A woman's going to be much more likely to take kindly to something that's pink."

Lester nodded at Lill and stood up tall as she kissed him on the cheek.

"That's for luck," said Lill, and Lester turned every shade of red. "You'll do fine."

Lester's mouth worked and worked like he was chewing on a big wad of Bobbi's bubble gum; he looked like he wanted to say something to Lill but couldn't make his lips move right. After a moment, he reached out and awkwardly shook Lill's hand like he and she had just signed a contract. Then, with one large pink Bible tucked under his arm, Lester strode from the bus wearing a sheen of confidence that fit him like a new pair of shoes. He walked stiffly, but with more pride than I'd reckoned him able to muster.

Lill bit her cuticles as she watched Lester through the window. Since we'd left Lincoln, she'd been coaching him, giving Lester tips on how to talk to people and how to present himself like a businessman, rather than just some deliveryman easily pushed around and disrespected. Now it was her turn to fidget and fret.

While Fish and Will pitched wadded-up balls of paper torn from Lester's stack of magazines at each other over the seats, Bobbi and I moved to sit by Lill. I didn't need to draw anything on Lill with my shiny silver pen to know that she was love-struck. I couldn't fathom it myself, but I guessed that happy endings came in all shapes and sizes.

Before long, Lester returned to the bus with a smile that threatened to split his face in two. Climbing up the three steep steps, he let out a whoop and a holler. Then, with a little heel-clicking skip, he leaned over and took Lill's face in his hands, laying a long hard kiss on her mouth. Lill threw her arms around Lester's neck and kissed him right back with a zest and a zing and a zeal that set the rest of us looking away—looking at just about anything, *anything* else.

Bobbi stuck out her tongue with a sour and shimmying shudder, squirming away from the happy couple and into the seat across the aisle, yet I couldn't help notice that lightning-fast smile of hers come and go once, like a sentimental chink in her teenage armor.

Loosening his lip-lock with Lill, Lester straightened up and announced, "Not only is the minister here accepting the delivery, but the Wymore Women's Guild would like to p-purchase three extra cases of Heartland B-Bibles."

Lill clapped her hands like my sister Gypsy, joyfully enthusiastic.

"That takes care of all the B-Bibles I didn't deliver yesterday," Lester said with relief, patting the back of his driver's seat as though now his bus was safe and he had been redeemed.

Lester recruited Fish and Will to help him carry boxes from the bus into the church. The boys tucked their heads down and held the boxes high to hide their faces as best they could, so that no one might recognize them from the ALERT! MISSING! ALERT! newscasts.

When they returned, Lester had cash and Fish and Will each had handfuls of powdered sugar donuts cut demi-semi into quarters. Will brushed white sugar off his black T-shirt as he handed me a piece of donut, then sucked more sugar from his fingers as he sat down next to me—next to me *close*. Despite the donuts, Fish looked dark as a storm cloud in his seat across the aisle and a shadow fell over the sun. Will glanced from Fish to Lester to me, looking worried.

"Lester says he has to make one more stop before we get to Salina, Mibs," he began. "I guess he has to give some gal money from selling all those Bibles, and the stop is right along the way. But he promised he'll get us down to the hospital soon—a few hours is all." Will was trying to reassure me. He knew how badly Fish and Samson and I wanted to get down to our poppa and was none too sure what might happen if we got more frustrated and impatient.

I held my bite of donut carefully between two fingers, watching the powder drop onto my lap as the bus rumbled and roared back to life. It was taking so long to get to Poppa; a few more hours of such uncertainty and dread were sure to feel long enough to hold days, months, or years worth of normal everyday worries—everyday worries like what to do about a certain curly-haired boy.

Will finished his donut and made a face, looking annoyed and uncomfortable. He reached under his leg and pulled out a wadded-up ball of magazine paper that he'd sat down on. Something about the crumpled ball of glossy paper caught my eye. I popped the piece of donut into my mouth and took the paper wad from Will, coughing a little as I inhaled the powdered sugar. Untwisting the crumpled ball, I smoothed it out against my lap, ignoring the way Will's knee kept bumping mine. The picture was the one from the magazine cover, the picture of the human heart looking like nothing more than a big mushy ball of watermelon threaded through with fine, pale roots. When I had first seen that picture, I had thought it made a person's heart look like a fragile, fragile thing rather than the sturdy muscle that I'd learned it to be. Now, I realized it was both.

With that thought in mind, I turned toward Will, my heart thumping, thumping, thumping hard against my ribs. I needed Will Junior's full attention. Scooting away from him a bit and setting the rumpled picture down between us, I reached out and took Will's face in my hands the way Lester had done with Lill. Holding another person's head in my hands like a basketball didn't feel near as awkward as I'd expected, despite how embarrassing it had been to watch Lester take hold of Lill the same way. But, unlike what happened between the two of them, there was to be no kissing this time around.

Instead, I looked Will straight in the eye, ignoring the way Fish goggled at us from the next bench over. Will looked back at me, startled, and I kept my heart muscle strong, feeling something inside me shiver like a pale green flower shoot just waking up for spring. But whatever that thing was, it was still too new to feel ready to bloom; it wanted time to send down roots. Someday soon I was going to bloom like crazy, and then I'd have what I needed to keep me standing tall.

"I like you, Will," I said. "I may even *like you* like you. But I'm just not ready to be kissing you yet, all right?" My heart was beating so hard with the hurly-burly fluster of truth-telling that it felt fit and full to bursting. I was confident that Will's heart was a steady one and suspected that he wouldn't fall to watermelon mush just because I wasn't ready to be kissing him. But we were friends now and I didn't want to bust that up.

I let go of Will's face and he stopped bumping my knee with his. His smile turned slaunchways and his black eye gave him a stubborn, scrappy look that I couldn't quite read all the way to the end.

"All right then, Mibs," he said. "Just give me the pen back."

"My birthday pen?" I asked, surprised and less muscled by measure. Will raised his eyebrows meaningfully and held out his hand. My stomach knotted and my lower lip began to tremble. I felt younger than young and all the rooting and all the growing up I'd just got done doing seemed to slip through my fingers as I reached down into the pocket of my special-occasion dress. I reached down past the paper-covered soap I'd so happily secreted there that morning and now, sadly, found broken in two. I reached down to wrap my hand around my fine and fancy happy birthday pen with its silver finger grip and its shiny rounded cap.

I couldn't look at Will as I held the pen out to him. I stared out the window instead, ignoring the satisfied look on Fish's face where he sat across the aisle and trying to stop my lips from quivering, trying to tell myself I was being a silly shilly-shally for feeling so let down when I'd just been the one *doing* the letting down. I watched rolling hills slip past and slope away like prairie waves outside the windows of the bus. I felt Will take the pen from my hand and heard him uncap it with a quick metallic *zing*.

A moment later, a voice filled my head like a deep-toned bell and the sound of it rang and echoed in my ears.

I can wait.

I can wait.

I can wait.

I turned back toward Will, who sat with his right hand raised in my direction like he was taking an oath or asking to be called on—a blue-inked sunshine smiling out at me from his palm.

"Don't worry, Mibs," he said aloud.

Chapter 28

AFTER WYMORE WE CONTINUED SOUTH, LEAVING Nebraska and finding ourselves on the far side of Kansas, still miles from Salina. Despite the Beaumont pleas to go straight to Salina Hope Hospital, Lester was fixed tight to his plans for one last detour. So we ate Pop-Tarts and chips and candy bars from the Mega Mega Mart and watched the landscape roll by outside the bus, trying not to think about Poppa lying broken in the hospital, trying not to imagine The Worst.

We were just north of Manhattan when a siren wailed and lights flashed behind us. All of us kids tensed like watch springs, coiling down into our seats, keeping low as Lester pulled the bus to the side of the highway with the rest of the Sunday traffic. It was with more than a touch of relief that we watched a white and blue police car fly past us on its way to someplace else and realized it wasn't ALERT! MISSING! ALERT! after us. But Lill and Lester hardly noticed a thing, so absorbed were they with each other.

Not long after, as Lester followed a long curve in the highway, Fish got to his feet and moved toward the front of the bus, stopping just shy of the yellow line painted on the floor. He was peering ahead of him up the highway and his knuckles were white where he clutched the back of Lester's seat. I got up from my place next to Will, squeezing past him to move toward Fish. Something was up, sure as sure.

"What's going on, Fish?" I asked him over the noise of the bus. The others were looking our way now, curious.

"I smell water," said Fish. "And lots of it." I cast a quick glance next to us at Lill, who was looking our way inquiringly. Lester turned his head as well.

"You've got a g-good nose," he said to Fish. "We're not too far from Tuttle Creek Lake. That's a fair-sized b-body of water, that is."

I put my hand on Fish's shoulder. "You're doing fine now, Fish," I reminded him quietly. "There's no need to worry . . . right? You've got things under control. You've got it scumbled."

Fish gave one quick, hard nod with each thing I said, as though he was punctuating my sentences with his chin.

"You're good," I said to him. "You told me so yourself back by the pool at the motel, remember? It's just a bunch of water."

Another nod.

"I'm good," he finally agreed, and his hand relaxed its grip on Lester's seat. I knew that, despite Fish's newfound confidence, the memories of his full-blown thirteenth-birthday hurricane would haunt him for a long, long time. It was the sort of thing no one could ever really forget.

"We're almost there," said Lester. "Carlene lives just

up ahead. As soon as I p-pay her what I owe her we can head on over to Salina. It won't be too long until you're all b-back with your families."

"Carlene? Not *Carlene!*" I yammered before I could stop myself. Startled, Lester swerved the bus into oncoming traffic, barely missing a honking pickup truck as he turned to look at me funny.

"What d'you know about Carlene, young miss?" asked Lester, surprised. "I don't b-believe I've ever mentioned her name. It's Carlene's cousin Larry that owns the Heartland Bible Supply Company. She helped me get my job."

"It's just . . . I . . . Isn't Carlene tattooed on your arm?" I said quickly, trying to cover up my blunder. I jabbed Fish in the ribs with my elbow. My brother's eyes went wide as he realized that I'd been hearing things about Lester that no one else had, and he tried to help.

"That's right, you've got tattoos on both arms, don't you?"

"Well, I did that a long time ago," Lester mumbled,

trying to unroll and button his shirtsleeves over his tattoos as he drove. His right shoulder began to jerk up and down like he was trying to keep a persistent bird or bee from landing on his shoulder. Lill looked away from him, studying her shoes.

"What's Lester still doing with all these rotten kids?" Rhonda's voice came spilling back into my head like vinegar.

"He's got no brains, that's the problem," Carlene's voice stirred in. I was disappointed to hear those ladies. For a while, Lester's mind had been too full of Lill to let those voices in; I hated to see him bid them back.

"Lester the dunderhead."

"Lester the dimwit."

"Lester the dumbbell."

"Lester the—"

"Stop it!" I cried out, and everybody looked at me. I realized I had my hands over my ears, and except for the noise of the bus, everything else was quiet.

"Why do you listen to them, Lester? Carlene

abandoned your dog on the side of the road because it chewed up her best red shoes!" I couldn't stand it anymore. Lester hit the brakes hard, steering the bus once again to the side of the road and coming to a sudden, lurching stop. He didn't look at me and he didn't move. Instead he just sat there, staring out the front window, letting the bus engine idle.

"She's a bad one, that Carlene," I said, then pressed my lips together tight, knowing I'd already said too much.

"Mibs, honey," said Lill softly. "Maybe you and Fish should just go sit back down."

"Naw, Lill," said Lester, his jaw quivering with anger or sorrow or both. "The girl's right. I don't know how or why she knows it, but she's right." He sniffed once and wiped his nose on his sleeve. "I always knew that C-Carlene got rid of my dog and lied about it. I just—she just—well, she g-got me this here job, after all." He traced the steering wheel in front of him with one finger. "She g-got me this bus."

"Lester the crybaby."

"Lester the softie."

"Lester the—"

"Go sit back down, Mibs," Lill repeated gently. Fish took me by the arm and steered me into a seat. Bobbi popped a gum bubble and raised her eyebrows my way, saying nothing but looking keen to my distress. Will sat on the edge of his seat, holding on to the bench in front of him as though ready to jump to my aid.

Lester let the bus idle at the side of the road for several minutes. I did everything I could to ignore Rhonda's and Carlene's raging abuse of Lester. I felt sick over his willingness to allow that kind of talk in his own head, and I vowed that I would never let Ashley Bing or Emma Flint or anybody else like them have that kind of power over me. I wouldn't let the voices of bullies or meanies or people who barely-hardly knew me work their way in to my brain and stick.

Eventually, Lester turned to Lill like a beaten-down man asking for mercy. "I just need to settle up with her, Lill. I just need to p-pay Carlene what I owe her from the B-Bibles and then I'm done, then I'm yours—if you'll have me, that is."

Lill's smile was so big that her whole large self seemed small in comparison. "Of course, Lester," she replied, and Lester's face transformed. He looked like a man who had finally found his own personal guardian angel.

"Then I am a happy man." The voice filled my head. And the voice was Lester's very own.

CARLENE TURNED OUT TO BE A big woman in a little woman's body. She had big hair, big teeth, big long fingernails, and big fuzzy slippers, but the rest of her was hollow and shrunken and bony. She looked like a witch dressed up for Halloween as a movie star. When Lester pulled the big pink Bible bus into the Tuttle Terrace Trailer Park, Carlene was sitting outside in a lawn chair. She was reading the Sunday paper and wearing nothing much more than a shiny satin robe and bright pink lipstick that bled into the wrinkles radiating from her lips, making them look ragged-jagged. Her feet were out of her slippers and I could see that her long, thick toenails were painted to match her lipstick.

When she saw the bus coming up her street, Carlene folded her paper and crossed her arms, not bothering to get up. I could see her squinting through the glare on the cracked windows at the rest of us, obviously surprised to find Lester carrying passengers.

"It's p-probably best if you all stay here," said Lester as he stood to descend from the bus. But before he could, Samson appeared at my side, squirming and wiggling and whispering into my ear. I grimaced at Fish as he looked our way, then called out to Lester as he opened the door of the bus.

"My brother's got to go to the bathroom, Mr. Swan, sir," I said. Fish smacked the palm of his hand to his forehead. Bobbi snorted and Will chuckled. Lester looked bewildered and anxious as he watched Samson silently dance in place in the aisle of the bus.

"You've got to take him, Lester," said Lill like they

were already an old married couple. Lester looked even more afflicted.

"I'll take him," said Bobbi, surprising everyone and standing up to take Samson's hand. "Someone's got to put the kid out of his misery." Samson took Bobbi's hand without hesitation and the two of them brushed past Lester to exit the bus. Not sure what was going to happen next, Fish and Will and I moved over to carefully slide open the windows facing Carlene's trailer so that we could have a better view of the action outside. Bobbi led Samson down the steps and stopped in front of Carlene's lawn chair.

"May we please use your bathroom, ma'am?" Bobbi asked plainly.

"Lester!" Carlene shouted, ignoring Bobbi as she stood up out of the lawn chair, dropping her newspaper and shoving her feet into her fuzzy slippers. "Lester, you stupid, senseless man! Get your scrawny butt down here right now and tell me what's going on! Who are all these kids?"

Samson clogged in place, tugging on Bobbi's arm. "Ma'am, please?" Bobbi repeated.

Carlene waved Bobbi off like a fly, rounding on Lester as he stepped down off the bus. Bobbi took the woman's wave as permission, whether it was meant that way or not, and hurried Samson up into the trailer to find the bathroom. It gave me the heebie-jeebies to watch Samson and Bobbi disappear into the house as though they were Hansel and Gretel stepping unknowingly into an enormous oven. Fish and Will must have felt the same way too; we all looked at each other and then barreled out of the bus, right past Carlene and Lester, following Bobbi and Samson up into the trailer and leaving Lill alone to wait things out.

The inside of Carlene's trailer was smoky and dim as the early-afternoon sunlight tried to force its way through the thick gauzy curtains that covered all the windows. The pungent odor of mothballs and scented candles flooded my nose and throat, making me cough. Carlene's furniture was garish and awful and every shelf or corner held tchotchkes and gewgaws and other tacky trinkets. Once Samson had finished taking care of his business, Bobbi and I took turns doing the same.

I stepped out of the bathroom just in time to catch Samson slipping beneath a long tablecloth that draped nearly to the floor, cascading over a small table just in front of the paneled bar that separated the living room from the kitchen. As he shimmied under the table, trying to disappear into this new hiding spot in his usual, stealthy way, I grabbed my brother by one ankle and pulled him out from under the table backward.

"Not now, Samson," I said. "Not here. Stay where we can see you, okay?" Samson looked back at me, his face as stony and expressionless as always, though I couldn't help but notice how his thin shoulders seemed to droop ever so slightly.

I was about to assure him that we'd be leaving soon, that it wouldn't be long until we were with Momma and Rocket down in Salina and that we'd soon be seeing

Poppa, but at that moment, Carlene burst into the trailer with Lester following at her heels.

Carlene was shouting and covering her ears. Lester was trying to hand her a wad of money clipped with a paper clip, but Carlene wouldn't even look at him. Ranting about Lester's lack of intelligence and general witlessness, she ushered Fish away from a shelf filled with animal figurines all made from jumbles of dry macaroni, and pulled a leaking, half-empty, *Sunny Miami* snow globe from out of Will Junior's hands.

"I'm not taking that money, Lester," Carlene hollered, glaring suspiciously at Bobbi, who was simply standing by the sofa. "I'm not taking it because it's not nearly enough. You come back here when you have twice that much." Carlene stopped talking just long enough to look around the room at each of us, her face twisted and contorted like she was trying to remember something, something that maybe *we* reminded her of.

"Fine, C-Carlene," said Lester. "Don't take the money. B-but just know that I won't *be* coming b-back, whether you take the money or not. I'm moving on."

"How dare you speak to me that way!" Carlene shouted, looking away from us kids and grabbing the money out of his hand greedily. The woman's temper flared hotter and she pitched the leaking snow globe straight at Lester's head. Lester ducked, then danced as Carlene began throwing other things at him as well; figurines and collector's plates sailed across the room, crashing against a wall or a lamp or a table as Lester jumped out of the way.

Both the flesh-and-blood Carlene and the Carlene inside Lester's head were screeching and bellowing so loudly that the voice of Rhonda could barely get a word in edgewise.

"I thought I raised you better than this, you idiot boy," Rhonda scolded him. *"Brawling with a woman!"*

"You are such a washout, Lester! Such a complete dud!" Carlene bellowed as macaroni poodles flew through the air.

"Lester's a moron . . ."

"Lester's a—"

"Shut—up!" At long last, it was Lester's turn to cover his ears and shout, his turn to tell all of the voices to be quiet. "That's enough!" Lester roared, standing tall in his overalls inside Carlene's trailer. "I've had enough of you, Carlene. I don't care if you get me fired—I'll find some way to keep my bus. I d-don't care about your cousin Larry, and I don't care about *you!*"

A shocked silence stopped up the room. For a moment, no one moved. No one breathed. No one spoke or even thought.

"Well, I'll never . . ." Rhonda started, then quickly faded out.

"Nitwit . . ." Carlene's voice inside Lester's head got in one final jab before it too sizzled out like a dying flame.

As the living, breathing Carlene stopped throwing things and stared at Lester, speechless for the first time, she remembered that she had an audience, as Bobbi, Fish, Will, and I all shifted in our places.

I had a bad feeling in the pit of my stomach and the little hairs on the back of my neck began to prickle. Carlene looked from one of us to the next several times, and I could see her slowly dawning recognition. It was time to go.

"Bless . . . my . . . stars. Lester, these are the kids on the TV," Carlene said low and slow like the first warning hiss of a poisonous snake. Lester looked from Carlene to the rest of us, obviously confused.

"The TV?" he repeated.

"The alert on the TV . . ." Carlene continued, stepping away sideways while keeping her eyes on us. "The missing kids. Land's sake, Lester! Did you help these kids run away?"

"W-what?" Lester stammered. "N-no . . . I mean yes. I mean—not on purpose, Carlene. Just l-let me explain!"

But Carlene was already reaching for the telephone. "You can explain yourself to the police, you defective dolt." She punched the buttons on the phone with one long, sharp fingernail.

"The p-police?"

"Not the police, Lester!" I shouted, running out from my corner of the room. I grabbed Lester's arm and tried to pull him to the door. "We have to get to Salina, Lester! Everything will be fine when we get to Salina, but we have to go *now*!" Bobbi, Fish, and Will all joined me in pushing-pulling Lester out of the trailer and back into the bus.

"We've got to go, Lester!" we shouted as we prodded him into the driver's seat and Will pulled the lever to close the door behind us. Lester moved slowly, like he was in a trance, starting up the bus and putting it in gear without hardly paying attention. His brain was still trying to catch up, trying to figure out if he was doing the right thing.

"What's happening?" Lill wanted to know, having stayed on the bus to give Lester some room to fight his own battles. But we spared no time for her on explanations.

"Just drive!" shouted Bobbi as Carlene stepped out of the trailer with her cordless phone to her ear, waving and pointing as though the operator on the other end of the line could see us driving away.

We were back on the highway, Lester sweating buckets and Lill's face drawn tight, bewildered and worried. Sitting on the edge of our seats, we kept watch out the windows for the first glimpse of flashing lights or the first sound of sirens on our tail. I remembered again that this was all my fault, that we wouldn't even be here if it wasn't for me and a savvy that had come and dropped me into hot water fast.

That hot water turned cold as ice as I stopped thinking about how sad and sorry my life had become and realized something even more terrible with the same sudden pain as a brain freeze. I stood up and looked around, and my heart skipped a beat.

"Where's Samson?"

"WHERE'S SAMSON?" I REPEATED FRANTICALLY. I stumbled to the back of the bus and turned over Lester's army cot. The others joined me, dumping out the bigger boxes and checking under every seat. But it was no use. Samson wasn't hiding anywhere on that bus. He simply wasn't there.

"We have to turn around!" we all started shouting. "We have to go back!" But Lester had his fingers knuckle-locked onto that steering wheel and was staring forward along the stretch of highway in front of him with the look of a man accepting the fact that his life was over and that he was probably going to end the day in prison for trying to do the right thing the wrong way. I felt bad, remembering my vow to keep Lill and Lester safe and out of trouble. But I couldn't sacrifice my own brother on that account; we couldn't *not* go back—even if the police were on their way.

Lill got to her feet and stood up tall between us kids and Lester as he continued driving away from the Tuttle Terrace Trailer Park.

"Just what's going on here, kidlings?" she wanted to know, calm but firm, her tone as parental as any mother's.

"Samson's not on the bus!" Fish shouted, and a gust of wind blew Lill's hair away from her face as the temperature and humidity began to rise perceptibly inside the bus. My brother set his jaw and clenched his fists, wrangling his savvy self before continuing. "Samson must still be at Carlene's. We've got to go back!"

Lill's eyes widened and she looked at us in shock. "We left the critter behind?" We all nodded at her mutely. Then Lill spun around toward Lester.

"Lester, turn the bus around!"

"B-but . . ." Lester stammered. "Carlene's called the police."

"It doesn't matter, Lester," Lill assured him, resting one hand on his nervous, shuddering shoulder. "We've got to go back."

Lester drove forward another quarter mile before he gave in. He made a wide-arcing U-turn faster than any old school bus should ever do, and for a moment I thought for sure that the big pink bus was going to tip right over. We all held on to whatever we could to keep from falling, and boxes of Bibles tumbled and slid.

We were nearing the trailer park when we heard the first siren in the distance. At the wheel, Lester had gone as pale as Gypsy's imaginary ghosts. The bright afternoon sun slipped behind thick dark clouds rising up from the distance, and the sky began to turn a funny shade of gray green. I remembered how close we were to that fair-sized body of water, Tuttle Creek Lake, and threw Fish a warning look.

"I'm fine," he barked at me through clenched teeth.

Nevertheless, I kept my eye on those clouds. Trouble was brewing.

Ignoring the sirens, Lester turned into the trailer park. He'd hardly gotten the door of the bus open before the rest of us, including Lill, blew right out like we were riding on a gust of Fish's wind. Lester followed on our heels, looking around him at the rising weather, at the trees bending and swaying, and at Carlene's lawn chair clattering down the street along with other rubbish picked up by the impending storm.

Carlene stood just inside her doorway. "The police are on their way, Lester," she shouted over the wind as we ran toward her through the first drops of rain.

"Where's Samson?" I demanded when I reached the woman. I could hardly catch my breath, I was in such a panic. "Where's my brother?"

Samson had to be inside. No one remembered seeing him leave the trailer. Bobbi and Lill moved toward the door, but Carlene blocked the way with her rawboned arms outstretched.

"This is my home and you are all trespassing," Carlene said, her pink lipstick sticking to her teeth as she sneered. The sirens were getting closer. Carlene smiled. "Left one behind, did you? Well, the boy is safe and sound and locked up tight until the officers get here."

"Locked up?" Lill boomed, her little voice growing as big as the thundering sky overhead. "Locked up? He's just a child!"

"Where is he, woman?" Lester demanded without a stutter or a stammer. The sky grew darker and darker and the wind sashayed in every direction, carrying the sound of the approaching sirens away and back. But Carlene just looked at us, smug and priggish, laughing at us with her eyes.

"You'll never find him," she said. "That one's got a knack for keeping hid, I can tell."

"You know where he is, don't you," Lester proclaimed, stating facts more than asking a question. Carlene just shrugged. Lill rose up to her full height, hovering like a heavenly avenger over the smaller woman; the look in her eyes was as fierce as the storm rising up from the lake, the storm that Fish was trying hard not to unleash in full.

But it was all just too much for my brother. His anger and worry got the best of him and he let loose with a blast of wind, directing it straight at Carlene, knocking her all the way to the far wall inside the entryway. We tumbled into the shaking trailer, leaping past Carlene to look everywhere for Samson. The first place I thought to look was under the long tablecloth over the table by the kitchen bar. But Samson wasn't there.

Everyone spread out, looking under the bed and behind the furniture. We checked in closets and cupboards. We dumped out the laundry basket and looked behind the drapes and the shower curtain. I even looked inside the oven—just in case. All the while, Fish's fury raged both inside and out, making the curtains thrash and wave, and setting every loose piece of paper and every stringy gray ball of dust flying through the air, his wrath threatening to pull the roof right off that old trailer.

I was searching the closet in the entryway as the first police car roared through the rain to stop behind the big pink Bible bus in a frenzy of multicolored noise. That was when a thought struck me. I knew how to get Carlene to tell me where Samson was.

All I needed was my pen.

Chapter 31

I REACHED DOWN DEEP INTO THE POCKET of my skirt, looking for my fancy silver happy birthday pen, but found only the broken, useless bar of paper-wrapped soap. I remembered that Will Junior still had it.

Will was searching the bedroom at the back of the house and I could hear Carlene in there with him, shouting at him to stop pulling all of the blankets off her bed.

Through a slim window set into the front door, I watched as two police officers stepped out of their patrol car and dashed through the rain toward the trailer. I quickly locked the dead bolt in the door and pulled a heavy chair in front of it to buy us more time, hoping that there might be another way out. Then I dashed down the narrow hallway toward the bedroom, passing the others on the way. Lester and Lill were in the kitchen looking again in all the cupboards. Bobbi was searching inside the washer and dryer. Fish was sitting on the floor in the bathroom with his head in his hands and his eyes squeezed tightly shut. He was struggling to keep that storm outside under control.

"It'll be all right, Fish! I know what to do!" I shouted to my brother, trying to reassure him as I ran past. Fish got up and followed me into Carlene's bedroom with Bobbi right behind him.

"Will! I need my pen!" I cried.

Will stopped a violent game of bedsheet tug-of-war with Carlene, letting go of his end so abruptly that the bony woman fell backward and landed in her now-empty laundry basket, her arms and legs flailing and kicking, one fuzzy slipper falling off, the other sailing through the air to hit the ceiling just over Bobbi's head—

Bobbi ducked to keep from getting hit. We were almost out of time. I could hear the police officers pounding on the front door.

"Will! My pen!" I thrust my hand out like a surgeon asking for a scalpel. Will dug deep into his own pocket and slapped the shiny pen into my hand, knowing exactly what I had in mind. We all shimmied around and over the bed, converging on the woman in the basket and trying to hold her down. Carlene started up such a noisy, hissing, spitting yowl, it was like trying to catch hold of a feral cat. The police pounded again on the door and I knew my time was up.

Carlene screamed, "Help! Help me!" So Fish blasted her with another whip of wind, making her flinch and turn her head aside, but it didn't stop her caterwaul.

"Help me! I'm being attacked!"

To shut the woman up, Bobbi pulled her roll of Bubble Tape from the pocket of her jeans, yanking a full arm's length of gum from the package and tearing it off. Quickly wadding the long ribbon into a tight tangle in her hand, Bobbi leaned forward and jammed the big gob of gum inside Carlene's open, roaring mouth, muffling the woman's shouts, at least momentarily.

Uncapping the pen, I grabbed for one of Carlene's kicking feet; it was the only part of her I could get close to.

"Lemme go!" the woman garbled around her enormous mouthful of sticky, juicy Bubble Tape, trying to spit it out but finding it difficult to dislodge the gum from her teeth. Kicking at me again, Carlene pulled her foot out of my grasp, her big hair flying up around her head like a mane as though the angry cat was turning into a lion.

"Try to keep her still," I shouted. "I only need a second!" As Fish and Bobbi struggled to pin Carlene's arms, Will grabbed hold of both of her feet. Carlene landed a rock-solid kick to Will's chest, knocking him backward against the bed, but he got up quickly and took hold of her feet with a tighter grip.

It took less than an instant—a dot, a dot, and a line—

just long enough to draw a simple face on the bottom of Carlene's cracked and calloused left foot.

"Where's my brother?" I demanded, trying to shut out everything except Carlene's voice inside my head, but finding it difficult to ignore the increasingly loud pounding at the front door and the sound of the rain now pummeling the metal siding of the trailer. "Where is he?" I repeated, shouting to Carlene, then pausing to listen for the single voice of her thoughts.

"He climbed in himself, the mangy, snooping little dog," the Carlene voice in my head replied as the two dots blinked above the scowling line of mouth. *"I just latched the panel so that he couldn't get back out."*

"What panel? Where is he?" I demanded, and for a moment Carlene stopped struggling, looking at me in surprise. "Where did Samson climb into himself?" I asked again.

Carlene finally managed to spit the thick, sticky mess of bubble gum from her mouth, sputtering it out so that it landed on the carpet near Fish like a piece of chewed-up meat. But she didn't start screaming again. Carlene didn't say a word. Instead she looked at me shrewdly, curiously.

"How did the girl know about the panel?" the inked face I'd drawn on Carlene's foot wondered in my head. Her eyes narrowed as she considered me carefully. The woman gave me the chills. It was almost as though she could read *my* mind, and for a moment I got scared. What if someone bad like Carlene ever found out about us Beaumonts and the things our savvies let us do? I hoped I'd never have to find out.

But before I could think any more about this new worry, I was distracted by a brand-new voice inside my head—muffled and distant like a hidden chime that seldom ever rings. The voice reminded me of . . .

"Samson!"

"I'm in the wall," the voice said in my head. Then it doubled. *"I'm in the wall—I'm in the wall."* As I listened, the seconds ticking by as I ignored Carlene and everyone else, I heard Samson's voice multiplying again and again

and again until it overlapped upon itself so many times that the words grew together into a gabble of chiming gibberish.

I'M IN THE WALL.
I'M IN THE WALL-I'M IN THE WALL.
I'M IN THE WALL-I'M IN THE WALL-I'M IN THE WALL-I'M IN THE WALL. I'M IN THE WALL-I'M IN THE WALL-I'M IN THE WALL-I'M IN THE WALL.
I'M IN THE WALL-I'M IN THE WALL.
. . . IN THE WALL.

I held up my hand as though trying to silence some of the voices, knowing that the others, including Carlene, were all watching me with keen interest.

"It's Samson," I said. "I can hear him. He says he's in the *wall*. What does that *mean?*" Everyone looked from me to Carlene, shocked and bewildered.

Fish roared at Carlene, sending her bushy mane of blond hair flying straight back and making her squint against his squall. "Tell us where he is!"

I didn't wait to see if Carlene answered. Dropping my pen and Carlene's ugly foot, I jumped up and shot out of the bedroom, following the volume of Samson's voice like a children's game of hot and cold, until I was standing again in front of the table that Samson had tried to climb under earlier. That was where his voice was loudest, but I had checked there already . . .

I'M IN THE WALL.
I'M IN THE WALL—I'M IN THE WALL.
I'M IN THE WALL—I'M IN THE WALL—I'M IN THE WALL—I'M IN THE WALL. I'M IN THE WALL—I'M IN THE WALL—I'M IN THE WALL—I'M IN THE WALL.
I'M IN THE WALL—I'M IN THE WALL.
. . . IN THE WALL.

I looked at the paneled wall of the bar directly behind the table and noticed now that the panels were uneven, overlapping one another like the sliding doors of a small closet. I hadn't realized that those panels could open.

The others had followed me into the living room and

watched now as I knelt on the floor by the paneled bar, banging on the boards and shouting to Samson as I tried to figure out how to slide them open. It only took me a second to find the latch and slide the first panel aside.

"He's here!" I cried out. "He's in here!"

There Samson sat, curled up—knees to chest—in the middle of an assortment of junk and debris. Old files and dusty shoe boxes were stacked around him inside the hidden storage space, along with bags of old clothes and a couple of broken-handled pots and pans.

Samson blinked at us from his hidey-hole lockup as though nothing out of the ordinary had happened. He was clutching a black plastic ballpoint pen that he must have found inside the storage area, and was using it to draw all over himself. Squiggles and doodles wiggled and jiggled up and down his arms, happy faces and stars, rocket ships, robots and bugs all decorated his skin, shifting and moving and prattling-tattling in that jumbled, jangling chorus inside my head.

I pulled Samson from out of the wall and hugged him

to me tightly, trying to listen to his thoughts. Allowed for once into my brother's inner world, I wished he hadn't drawn on himself quite so much—I couldn't make sense of all the noise. But I was so glad to see him, I could think of little else. Samson's mishmash medley inside my head was like beautiful music.

As soon as we'd found Samson, everyone converged on us at once—

Lester and Lill appeared around the corner from the kitchen, looking relieved—

Carlene came out of the bedroom hoisting a broom that she pointed our way, as though she planned on sweeping us all out of her home, or maybe on jumping aboard and flying off into the storm—

And on top of the rest, the police chose that moment to kick down the door.

Chapter 32

THE NEXT HOUR WAS SHEER CHAOS. Additional police cars arrived on the scene just moments after the first drenched and dripping officers smashed into Carlene's trailer. Investigators poured through the house, as well as through the Heartland Bible Supply bus. As the rain stopped and the skies cleared, nosy neighbors, all home and glad for some real-life entertainment in the midst of their quiet Sunday afternoon, spilled into the street to watch the storm blow over and the drama unfold. Someone took away Carlene's broom, and all three adults—Lester, Lill, and Carlene—were taken outside to talk to the officers. A child welfare caseworker, a middle-aged woman wearing gray slacks and flat shoes, stood over us kids protectively. People kept talking all around, but the voices were all outside of my head, so I could tune them out; I could turn them off and just concentrate on Samson.

Bobbi, Will, and Fish were all seated next to one another on Carlene's sofa. Bobbi slouched back against the cushions doing her best impression of a bored teenager, popping and snapping a new length of chewing gum, obviously annoying the caseworker, while Will watched the comings and goings of all of the officers intently. Fish looked pale; his storm had settled down as soon as we'd found Samson, but trying to scumble it had left him weary and worn out.

Samson and I sat on the floor in front of the others, leaning against the front of the sofa. Samson's ink-covered hand rested in mine; he was still clinging tightly to his ballpoint pen. Every now and then I'd catch a word or phrase amidst the jumble of his thoughts, but as nonsensical and sweet-toned as it all was, his voices soon settled into a soothing kind of background melody.

Soon, paramedics joined the crowd, offering us blankets and water and checking each of us over; asking a lot of questions and photographing Will's black eye and Fish's scratched face.

We tried to explain again and again what had happened as people jotted notes into notepads. I tried to tell the officers and the caseworker and the paramedics that it was all my fault that we'd run away. I tried to tell them how terribly important it was that we get to Poppa—get to Poppa soon! All those precious minutes ticking by were minutes with him we were wasting.

"I'm responsible!" I repeated in exasperation. "It was *my* idea to go down to Salina. My idea to sneak onto the bus. It was even my idea to trick Lill into thinking we'd called home," I said. The adults listened in their adult way and nodded and uh-huh-ed and a-ha-ed. But I never really felt convinced that any of them believed me . . . and I hadn't even mentioned my savvy.

I was afraid that things were going downhill fast for

Lester and Lill, and I felt sick to my stomach with worry for them and ashamed about our lies and deception. I hadn't done a very good job of taking care of them.

The future didn't look too bright for Carlene either—what with her locking Samson into her storage space and all. But I didn't trouble myself as much with her. She was just a nasty, rotten apple.

"Do you know anything about our poppa?" I asked the caseworker in the gray slacks, hoping that she might know something. "Will we get to see him soon?" But the woman just offered us a sorry, practiced smile and shook her head. No matter what or who I asked, all I ever heard was "We don't know yet" or "That's being sorted out" or worse, "Please just sit quietly and let the officers do their job."

The hubble-bubble was far from over. Kansas state troopers had begun to arrive, adding two additional vehicles to the already jammed-up and puddled street outside. From where I sat, I could see them through the busted-down door. I was beginning to think that we were *never* going to make it to Salina. It looked more and more like arrangements were being made for Pastor Meeks and Miss Rosemary to come and pick us all up in Manhattan to take us back with them to Hebron. I couldn't let that happen. We'd come too far to go home now.

One of the troopers got out of his shiny silver car in a hurry, not even bothering to put on his funny, dented hat. He raced up the short walk toward the trailer. His dark hair was clipped shipshape short and his young face was pulled tight with misgiving. The officer looked familiar, and I recognized him as just an older, more shaved-and-muscled version of Will Junior. This man must be Will and Bobbi's brother, Bill.

I've never seen such a look of relief on anyone as I saw then, when Bill found us all sitting in the living room safe and sound.

"Bill!" shouted Bobbi, jumping up with Will as soon as they saw the man coming. Bobbi rushed forward to wrap her arms around her older brother's chest. Will stood back a bit self-consciously.

"You okay, Roberta?" asked Bill.

"Yeah, I'm fine," she answered, letting go and stepping back.

As soon as Bill released Bobbi, he grabbed Will to him in a big bear hug and looked as though he wasn't ever planning on letting go. He held on and on.

"What were you thinking, kid?" I heard Bill whisper affectionately. "Were you looking for trouble like your old man used to get into? Don't try to be like me, Will. You're too smart for that."

It took me a moment to adjust my understanding of things. It appeared that I might have been wrong as wrong in believing that Will Junior was Bobbi's brother.

Will had a secret. Now I knew his secret.

It occurred to me that Bill must have been mighty young when Will was born. I could just picture Miss Rosemary, with her need to make all things spick-and-span and apple-pie, taking over the raising of her own grandson. At least it finally made Will *Junior* make some sense.

When Bill finally let go of his son, the man was wiping tears from his eyes, struggling to regain his state trooper composure, and I saw my chance to finally tell my story to someone who might listen.

"Officer Meeks? . . . Uh, Mr. . . . Bill . . . sir?" I had no idea of the right thing to call this man, but as he turned his attention to me, I struggled on, knowing that I had to stand up tall for Lill and Lester, stand up tall and pull them out of the stew I'd put them in. "Sir, you've just got to believe me—this is all my fault! I just wanted to see my poppa!" And with that, I burst into tears.

ONCE I'D BEGUN TO CRY, SITTING on the floor of that dim living room, still sixty miles from Salina Hope Hospital and Poppa and Momma and Rocket, I couldn't stop. It wasn't pretty, delicate crying either. It was full-on, snot-dripping, chest-wheezing, jibber-jabber wailing. Will stepped away from his daddy to kneel down and take my hand in his. Samson leaned up against me. The child welfare caseworker walked over to the bathroom and retrieved a box of tissues, but every one I pulled from the box smelled of mothballs and Carlene, which made me cry all the harder.

"You must be Mississippi Beaumont," said Bill gently.

"She likes to be called 'Mibs,' Dad," Will asserted, coming to my rescue.

Bill pulled a chair over by me and sat on its edge. "Is that right, Mibs?" he asked.

I gave a big sobbing nod, trying to calm myself down so as not to give the very worst possible first impression. I noticed Bill looking at Will's hand on mine, and for a minute Officer Meeks looked done-in and young as young.

"You've been through a lot these last few days," Bill said gently, making me want to bawl even more. "I know your dad's over there in the hospital in Salina, and I know you probably just wanted to go find him, right?"

Another big sobbing nod.

"Then maybe we should go do just that."

Everyone looked up at Bill Meeks as though wondering if they'd heard him right. Even the caseworker looked startled.

"Officer, you can't—" the caseworker started saying, but stopped as Bill looked up at her firmly.

Bill asked the caseworker to give us a little room to talk. He wanted to hear our whole story from top to bottom firsthand. We all joined in on the telling as the caseworker took a seat along the wall. Bill listened keenly and without interrupting, occasionally running his hand across his razor-short hair.

When we'd finished our tale, Bill sat there for a time without saying anything.

"Is our poppa okay?" a small voice fell like a pebble into the stillness, rippling the tension in the air like deep water. With Samson's hodgepodge of thoughts already streaming incoherently through my brain, it took me a moment to realize that he had spoken aloud. I tried to swallow, but found my throat was too rough and too tight as I waited for the man's answer.

Officer Meeks shook his head. "I haven't heard anything recent about your dad, but I'll see what I can find out. I need to talk to some people here and figure out what's going to happen next. You kids wait here. I'll be back in a few minutes." He stepped away to converse with the officers outside. As I watched him go, I couldn't help but wonder if Bill's hair grew out curly like his son's, and the last of my tears dripped off my chin, leaving me red-eyed and headachy. I could see Bill talking to Lester, talking to Lill, and then talking to Carlene. I could hear a clock tock-ticking slowly somewhere in the kitchen, like its battery was running low or like it too was holding its breath, waiting to see what would happen.

After finishing with Carlene, then speaking with several other officers, Bill spent a long, long time on a cell phone before coming back into the trailer with a stiff-necked, hard-shell look about him. He didn't sit back down in the chair, but stood over us instead, looking lawful and steady in his crisp uniform, with his badge and his gun and his trooper face on. He spoke first to me and Fish and Samson, his words sounding practiced and formal, yet his tone was round-cornered and kind.

"I'm very sorry to tell you that your father's condition hasn't improved. He's—well, he needs his family around him now. It's important that we get you down to Salina soon."

Fish slid off the couch to sit on the floor on the other side of Samson. "We have to be strong for Poppa now," he said, putting one arm around our little brother, and squeezing my shoulder once as he did. As worn out as Fish was, only the faintest of breezes blew through the room, and since the door to the trailer was still smashed in, nobody took much notice of a little bit of wind. Samson merely nodded silently, but his overlapping voice in my head grew busier and less musical, like a flock of nervous geese. I still couldn't make out one thought from another—loud as he was thinking, my littlest brother's innermost self was still a mystery, even to my savvy self.

Bill Meeks paused before continuing. When he did speak again, it was to all five of us. "You kids have caused more than a little trouble in the last twenty-four hours. A lot of people spent a great deal of time and energy looking for you, and you gave your families a huge scare." Bill looked at us long and hard, until we all felt ready to crawl beneath the trailer and stay there. Then he took a deep breath through his nose and smiled sympathetically, giving Will a quick conspiratorial wink before continuing on in a lower voice, glancing at the caseworker sitting along the wall.

"I know how easy it is to make wrong choices and end up in difficult situations, but things don't always turn out badly. There will be consequences, of course, but no one got hurt, and no hurt was meant. So, as far as I know, no one's pressing any charges against those folks out there. Mr. Swan and Miss Kiteley may have made some ill-advised decisions, but they did do a good job of looking after you and keeping you all safe."

"Lester and Lill aren't going to go to jail?" I said, looking up at Will's dad.

"No, Mibs, they're not going to jail." Bill's smile widened. "In fact, I kind of need their help right now."

"You do?" said Bobbi.

"Well, I need *someone* to drive you all over to Salina,

don't I? It would be a tight fit in the patrol car, and it seems Lill and Lester would really like to see you get there."

I was flooded with such relief that I almost started crying again. Lester and Lill were going to be safe, and I would soon be with my family. I wanted to thank Bill Meeks from the bottom of my mush-and-muscle heart, but I could find no words. For the first time, I wished that my savvy worked in reverse. I wished that all I had to do was draw a smiling face somewhere on my skin, so that others might know how I was feeling without me having to say a thing. But, from the way Bill was looking at me, I had the feeling he knew anyway.

The child welfare caseworker, still not entirely certain Bill's plan was sound, insisted on riding along with us on the big pink Bible bus and requested that an armed officer be aboard as well. While Lester welcomed us kids back onto his bus without a grudge, the idea of having the extra official passengers on board made him fidget.

"It will be okay, Lester," Lill soothed. "I'll stay by you in the front seat. We can talk about your next delivery, if you'd like. Maybe we can even talk about starting up your very own Bible-selling business."

"My own b-business, Lill?" Lester said in surprise, now clearly distracted from the fact that there was a police officer climbing onto his bus.

"Why sure, Lester," she said. "I know you've got it in you."

"What took you so long to come into my life, Lill?" Lester said with a sigh, shaking his head and staring at his feet. "I wish I c-could have met you years ago."

"I'm always late, Lester," Lill laughed. "It's just a talent I can't escape."

I watched Lill calm Lester's worries and thought about how good and kind she was, and about all the trouble I'd caused her. But while Lill didn't seem to hold our deception at the motel against us, she did want to know how we'd managed it.

"You kids are too smart for your own good," Lill

said after we'd said our sorries and explained how we'd faked the call to Miss Rosemary. Lill hugged each of us to her in turn. "The world had better watch out for all of you. You're big trouble in the making."

Bill was going to drive ahead of the Heartland Bible Supply bus as an escort all the way to Salina and he asked Will if he wanted to ride along. Poor Will contemplated the patrol car, looking torn in two. I imagined that he'd love nothing more than to ride up front in that car with his daddy, like he was a state trooper himself. But then Will glanced at me.

"Next time?" he said to his dad with a sheepish grin.

"Go on with your friends," laughed Bill, rumpling Will Junior's hair, then pulling him toward him for another back-thumping hug.

"I guess you've been missing your poppa too," I said to Will as we got settled.

He shrugged, and squeezed my hand tight. "Things don't always happen the way you want them to, Mibs," he said. I thought about that and I thought about my own poppa in the hospital. I thought about the way my savvy hadn't worked out in the way I'd hoped or how our journey to Salina had taken its own twists and turns. Then I remembered what Lill had said just before falling asleep in the motel the night before. *You never can tell when a bad thing might make a good thing happen.* I realized that good and bad were always there and always mixed up together in a tangle. Though, at the moment, I wasn't sure that made me feel any better.

THE CLOSER WE GOT TO SALINA, the greener the world became, as rolling prairie transformed into rich, irrigated farmland. As soon as we'd found Samson behind the paneled wall in Carlene's trailer, Fish's storm over Tuttle Creek Lake had dissolved. Now the crisp white light of spring sunshine opened up the skies once more. But despite the sunshine and the brilliant green landscape, my thoughts were bleak and barren and black-and-white. All I could think about was Poppa.

Will Junior and I sat near the front of the bus so that he could keep watch on his daddy's patrol car, and Fish and Bobbi were across the aisle, ignoring the caseworker just behind them. Bobbi was chewing her gum, and painting her nails with red Mega Mega Mart nail polish, cursing softly at every bump in the road, and Fish was leaning up against the window with his eyes closed. I knew he wasn't asleep. I figured he was thinking about Poppa, same as me. I couldn't get Officer Meeks's words out of my head. I couldn't forget what he'd said about Poppa.

He needs his family around him now. It sounded terrifying to me. It sounded hopeless.

Not being able to get past the officer stationed at the back of the bus, Samson had curled up in the front seat with Lill, his head in her lap. Lill was using all of the alcohol wipes from the new first aid kit to scour away the black ink from Samson's arms and hands. That ink burbled and shivered as it came off, paring down the mayhem in my head into a single pointed voice that pierced my heart before being scrubbed away.

Strong for Poppa.

Strong for Poppa . . .

We had one last stretch of interstate to travel, a slow clip-clop countdown of miles and exits, and I had to bite my tongue to keep myself from asking, "How much farther? How much farther? How much farther?"

It seemed like an hour longer than forever before Lester followed Bill Meeks's patrol car off the interstate at exit 252, passing a sign with a large white *H* that told us we were on the right path to the hospital. I trembled at the sight of that stark, bone-white letter. It meant we were almost there, almost to Poppa at last.

With a left turn that took us under the interstate and onto Ninth Street, Bill led the bus into the town of Salina. The signal lamps at every intersection had been blasted out, looking now like upright rows of empty eye sockets. Cars crept and crawled across the busier streets, and traffic was backed up, even though it was Sunday afternoon. Crews were out trying to replace all of the broken red, yellow, and green glass, and the city was obviously still struggling to recover from Rocket's electric wake. I swallowed hard; I'd never seen Rocket make such a mess. It made me shiver all the more. Maybe it hadn't been such a good idea for him to take Momma to Salina after all. I hoped that the hospital had plenty of spare lightbulbs and that Rocket wasn't getting too close to any of the important, life-saving equipment.

We were all sitting up on the edge of our seats now, any last trace of drowsiness having vanished as soon as we got off the interstate. Without Bill leading the way, it would have taken forever to maneuver through the jammed streets. But Bill turned on his siren, and even got out once or twice to direct the bus through intersections where frustrated drivers wouldn't let us pass. The afternoon sky, arcing blue as cornflowers over the town before our arrival, was now beginning to cloud over. Precipitation gathered from the corners of the atmosphere to take the shape of a small dark storm cloud directly over the bus. But Fish held tight to his savvy with a strong and skillful scumble, and the cloud simply hovered grimly overhead, sending down neither a sprinkle nor a spatter.

Bill must have called ahead to announce our arrival, for as soon as the big pink Heartland Bible Supply bus followed his patrol car into the hospital's parking lot, stopping right in front of the large sliding glass doors of the entrance, we saw our families waiting for us.

Pastor Meeks and Miss Rosemary appeared to be struggling between relief and anger, their faces going slack, then rigid; smiling, then stiff. Rocket and Momma were there too, looking haggard and sleepless. To my surprise, Momma was hanging on to a squirming Gypsy, and Grandpa Bomba was leaning on Rocket's arm, holding tight to one of Grandma Dollop's jars. The pastor and his wife must have brought the rest of our family down with them, and I was grateful to them. It was going to be good to have everyone in the family together again.

As soon as Lester opened the door of the bus, Momma set Gypsy down, taking her by the hand and rushing forward as we all began to climb down those three steep steps.

"Where in the world have you all been? What were you thinking?" Momma cried as she grabbed Fish and Samson and me and held on tight, tight, tight, crushing us together along with Gypsy, like a big bouquet of flowers in a perfect hug. When at last she let go, she pulled us inside, fussing over each of us as if she were checking for any missing fingers or toes.

"I wasn't worried," Rocket said, his face so lined and hardened that I knew not to believe him. He gave me a sideways shoulder squeeze and an unintentional electric shock that made me jump. His voice cracked as he said, "Savvy birthdays always tend to cause a rumpus." Then he punched Fish on the arm and mussed up Samson's hair, leaving it standing on end and crackling with static. It hadn't occurred to me until then that Rocket hadn't only been worried for Poppa, he'd been worried about us as well. Guilt nearly crushed me—no wonder he'd caused so much damage.

Grandpa Bomba stood, tears streaking his wrinkled face as he looked from each of us to the next. He held the glass jar with its faded label tucked into the crook of his arm, and I knew immediately which one it was.

I threw my arms around my old grandpa, hugging him as hard as his ancient bones could bear. "It's okay, Grandpa," I said. "We're all together again just the way we should be."

Letting go, I turned back to Momma. Samson was at her side, tugging on her shirt. Ignoring Gypsy as she tried to pull her hand free, Momma bent down so that Samson could whisper in her ear. Samson's eyes were round and dark as he looked up into our momma's face and I could see his lips form the word that was on all of our minds.

"Poppa?"

Momma's face drooped, the warm smile she'd greeted us with vanishing for a half second before being replaced with a very different kind of smile—the kind of smile born from love and sorrow and the desire to protect us all from our very worst fears.

"It's good you're all here now," Momma said softly.

"It was a mistake for me not to bring you with me in the first place."

"But, Momma," I said. "You don't make mistakes."

Momma's face pinched and tightened as she tried not to cry. "Oh Mibs," she said, pulling me to her again. "I can make awfully perfect mistakes."

Rocket dropped his head and stared at the floor, his knuckles white and his jaw clenched as the lights in the waiting room dimmed and pulsed once but did not burn out or shatter.

"I'll let you all say your good-byes," Momma said, letting go of me and wiping her eyes. "Then we'll go up to see Poppa."

"Let's just go now," implored Fish, picking up Gypsy and grabbing Momma's arm.

But Momma stood firm. Running a hand absently through Fish's messy hair, she continued, "Nothing will change in the next two minutes, Fish. You can say good-bye to your friends."

A sobbing wail drew my attention. Nearby, Miss

Rosemary was trying to rein in her dripping tears. She dabbed her eyes with a white handkerchief and took turns squeezing Will and Bobbi to her, while Pastor Meeks kept his eyes closed and his hands clasped together, looking as though he might be sending up a silent and mighty prayer of thanks.

Bill had joined us all inside the waiting area, hanging back a bit during the emotional family reunion—watching keenly as Miss Rosemary clucked over Will's black eye like a mother hen. But when Pastor Meeks finished his prayer and opened his eyes, he reached out a hand, giving Bill's a firm shake and pulling him into the group with a hearty thump on the back.

As soon as Bobbi could, she detached herself from her mother and sidled closer to Rocket with a smile, looking at the way my brother's T-shirt stuck to him with static. Rocket noticed Bobbi's smile quick enough, and despite everything, he managed a half smile back her way. I remembered the way she'd talked about my brother in the pool, and watched to see what Bobbi might do.

"Hey, Rocket," said Bobbi, pushing her bangs out of her eyes and shifting her weight onto one hip.

"Hey, Bobbi," said Rocket with a nod, a stray spark of blue popping at his fingertips.

Bobbi noticed that spark even if no one else had. Smiling wider and raising her eyebrows, she pulled the gum from out of her mouth and stuck it on the back of a nearby chair without taking her eyes off my oldest brother, as though getting herself ready to kiss him then and there, while she had the chance.

But before Bobbi could say or do anything more, Miss Rosemary grabbed hold of her daughter's arm and pulled her away from the rest of us. Miss Rosemary's tears shut off like a faucet and she railed, "You're in enough trouble already, Roberta. Don't go asking for more." Then she looked at us Beaumonts as though we were devil angels sent to lead her children astray.

The shiny gold minivan was parked outside and all Miss Rosemary wanted to do was restore her life to the proper order and get back on the road to Hebron with Bobbi and Will in tow.

Lester and Lill were standing in the open doorway of the bus, peering past the sliding glass doors of the hospital to watch the reunion inside with broad smiles on their faces. Lester stood on the step behind Lill with his hands on her shoulders, and I could tell just by looking at them that they were going to be all right. But I hoped, hoped, hoped I'd get a chance to see them both again someday. It wouldn't seem right not to.

I'd made it to Salina; I was finally there. Even so, I had a feeling in my chest like my heart was breaking up, like it was turning into nothing more than a big ball of melon that could dissolve into little watery chunks at any moment. It felt disjointed and downside-up to be parting ways so abruptly with all my new friends. All I could do was wave to Bobbi and Will as the preacher's wife dragged them out of the hospital.

Just before the sliding doors slid shut, Will caught my eye with his own quick wink. I realized I'd be seeing him again at church next Sunday, or I hoped I would—I hoped you couldn't get kicked out of church for making bad choices, or for knowing you'd probably make those same choices again if you had it all to do over. I hoped that God could understand my reasons for doing what I'd done better than Miss Rosemary had.

Before following his wife out of the hospital, Pastor Meeks shook Momma's hand. He shook Grandpa's and Rocket's too. "You'll all be in our prayers," he said, with a stern nod to the rest of us.

"Thank you, Pastor Meeks," Momma said to the preacher, trying to suppress a wistful smile as the man's hair filled up with Rocket's static, standing straight up off his head.

As soon as the older man turned to leave, Officer Bill Meeks stepped toward us. "You kids stay safe and keep out of trouble, all right?" Then Bill shook hands with each of us, even Gypsy, before he left. At the door, he looked over his shoulder at me, and nodded once before following the preacher out of the hospital. I watched

Bill through the clear glass doors as he stopped briefly to exchange words with Lester and Lill, then strode over to say his own good-byes to Bobbi and Will as they climbed up into the minivan. I liked Bill Meeks, and I was glad that Will wanted to grow up to be just like *this* daddy.

On the Heartland Bible Supply bus, Lester's shoulders began to twitch. He was ready to be on his way. Lill blew us a kiss, and Fish and Samson and I all waved back at her.

At last, it was time to go find Poppa.

INSIDE THE ELEVATOR ON OUR WAY up to the critical care unit on the fourth floor of the Salina Hope Hospital, Momma squeezed us all to her once again, kissing each of us on the top of the head.

"We've been so worried," was all she could manage to say and still keep her voice under control. Hooking one arm through Fish's and holding my hand in hers while Rocket wrangled both Gypsy and Grandpa Bomba, Momma tucked Samson up under her wing as though by keeping us close enough, we might not disappear again.

Rocket stared my way like he was examining me

for new spots or stripes. He looked me over head to toe and back again. "How'd your birthday treat you, Mibs?" he finally asked, just as the elevator doors opened up on the fourth floor. For a moment we all just stood there. We knew Rocket wasn't asking about my cake or my party or even my runaway journey through the heartland.

Momma looked at me anxiously, as though, having been steeped in all of her other worries, she'd almost forgotten about my savvy. The elevator door began to close again with all of us still standing inside, but I reached out and caught it with my hand.

"It treated me just fine, Rocket," I answered as though I hadn't had a single lick of trouble. "I believe that me and the world will survive my savvy, once I get a bit more used to it, that is."

Glancing at the nurses' station just across the hall, Momma said, "I want to hear all about everything. I want to know about your savvy, Mibs," she said quietly. "And about everything that's happened to you since we last saw you. You have to tell me the whole story, from start to finish—all of you."

"First Poppa?" whispered Samson, tugging again on Momma's sleeve.

Momma smiled the saddest smile I'd ever seen. Her smile was perfectly heartbreaking. Unable to speak, she nodded, tears filling up her blue, blue eyes. Stepping off the elevator, Momma led us toward the nurses' station. The nurses all looked up from their coffee and their charts, smiling at Momma and Grandpa and the rest of us like they were saying sorry, sorry, sorry—sorry that your poppa's hurt, sorry that he's broken.

"Are these the rest of your children, Mrs. Beaumont?" asked a nurse wearing bright blue scrubs dotted with little rainbows.

"Yes," said Momma. She nodded quickly toward Fish and Samson and me. "These three are my delinquents—my wandering adventurers."

"We were just trying to get down here, Momma," I said plaintively. "I just had to see Poppa. I *had* to."

Momma nodded. "I know, Mibs." Then, turning back to the nurse, she asked, "Can I take my children in to see their poppa now? Because I honestly can't predict what might happen if they don't get to see him soon."

"Yes, Mrs. Beaumont," said the nurse with a kindly nod. "You can take them in."

Momma led us across the hall, toward a half-open door, passing a maintenance man on a ladder who was cursing to himself as he replaced a long fluorescent light in the ceiling. Stopping with her fingers wrapped around the door handle, Momma looked each of us in the eye as though she was reeling us in to her, trying to hold us close with her gaze.

"Momma?" said Fish, with just a trace of wind blowing the hair out of his eyes. "Poppa hasn't woken up yet?"

"Not yet, Fish," Momma said. "Not yet." Then, sharing a sorrowful knowing look with Grandpa and taking a deep breath, she continued slowly, choosing each word carefully. "The doctors say—well, they say he may not." Then she added quickly, "But we will keep hoping and praying, because, if nothing else, those are things we can all do."

I felt as though the earth was going to open up and swallow me, and I wondered if Grandpa was shaking the ground or if it was only my legs quaking beneath me.

Momma looked quickly toward Fish, past experience readying her for his storm. But aside from a smattering of rain against the windows just beyond the nurses' station, Fish was holding it together. I suppose it could have been the numbing shock of Momma's words that dampened Fish's savvy, or even Samson's hand in his—perhaps it was Fish's own brand-new scumbling strength, but standing there outside Poppa's room, not even a breeze tickled the air.

Momma looked then at Rocket.

"I'll be okay," he reassured her, "I can go in this time. Please, Momma? It will be worse if you make me stay out."

Casting her glance from the man on the ladder to stray shards of glass missed by the last sweep-up of the hard tiled floor, Momma didn't look convinced. But Rocket's eyes pleaded with her, and she gave in; I knew she wanted our whole family together at last.

Finally, her glance fell on me. "Is there anything I need to know, Mibs, before we go in?"

I shook my head. "Nothing," I whispered. "There's nothing." How I had hoped that this moment would come and I would find the power to wake up Poppa, to rescue him and bring him back home to us in Kansaska-Nebransas. But like the color of my eyes or the size of my feet, my savvy wasn't something I had any say over. Just like everyone else, I could do nothing, nothing, nothing for Poppa now.

With one last look at her extraordinary family, Momma pushed the door to Poppa's room all the way open, and we filed in quietly to find Poppa resting, looking nothing at all like Sleeping Beauty.

Chapter 36

AT FIRST, POPPA DIDN'T EVEN LOOK like Poppa. His bald head was wrapped round and round with bandages. He had wires and tubes and machines to help him do everything, and his face was pale and sagging. Every one of us found another person's hand to hold as we stepped closer to Poppa's bed. He had a tube in one arm and a blood pressure cuff wrapped around the other. Wires and sensors were attached to him everywhere and his pointing finger looked like it had a big fat clothespin on it. Poppa's arms rested outside his blankets; his hands lay palms-up like he was reaching out for help.

I felt as though I'd forgotten how to breathe. The normal, simple act of filling and emptying my lungs became the hardest thing I'd ever had to do. I was afraid to swallow, knowing that it would unleash the flood of tears that burned behind my eyes.

Grandpa Bomba struggled with the lid of the jar in his old hands, his knobby fingers unable to get a good strong grip as he tried to open it. Tenderly, Rocket took the jar from Grandpa and gently tapped the lid against the bedside table once or twice. Then he loosened the lid a half of a turn, and Momma and Poppa's never-ending love song spilled loudly into the room. Momma took the jar from Rocket, tightening the lid a quarter-turn to lower the volume, and keep the nurses from rushing in to shush us. But her hands trembled as she did it.

I rubbed my knuckles gently against Poppa's jaw, feeling the scratchy stubble of his unshaven chin; then I dropped my hand to his arm. I ran my shaking hand lightly down Poppa's arm and stopped with one finger pressed against the inside of his wrist as though checking for a pulse. In that moment, I couldn't help remembering the homeless man by the Dumpster behind the Emerald Truck Stop Diner and Lounge. That man had been asleep too. Asleep and totally alone. Totally hopeless. He'd had no one to play songs for him, no one to listen, no one to care. But Poppa had all of us, and we would never let him go.

"Mibs," said Fish, hardly loud enough for me to hear. I looked up at my brother, who tapped his own forearm meaningfully, then nodded at Poppa. "Miss Mermaid, Mibs," he whispered. "What about Miss Mermaid?" Samson looked at me then too, his dark eyes round.

I could not believe that I'd forgotten. How could I forget about Poppa's faded navy tattoo? How could I have forgotten Miss Mermaid?

Gently, careful not to bump any important tubes or wires, I turned Poppa's arm around. There she was, wrapped around her anchor, winking beneath the hair on Poppa's arm. But to my distress, even Poppa's tattoo looked belly-up and lifeless, like that long-haired mermaid had dodged a shipwreck to get washed up on dry land.

I listened hard for that mermaid's voice inside my head. I traced her long green tail with the tip of my finger. Then I closed my eyes tight and tried to hear what Poppa might be thinking, what Poppa might be feeling, what Poppa might be dreaming or wishing or knowing. I listened and listened and listened.

But there was nothing. No voices in my head. No Poppa at all. I heard the rasp of metal against glass as Fish, face scrunched up against his tears, reached out to close the lid all the way on Grandma Dollop's jar, stopping short the never-ending love song; I wasn't sure if he closed the jar to help me hear Poppa, or to keep all of our hearts from tearing into pieces. Without that song, so much stillness filled the room that I felt as broken and dark as all of Rocket's busted lightbulbs.

I realized that Fish and Samson were still looking at me, hardly breathing. They were watching me listen. They wanted to know what I could hear—wanted to know what Miss Mermaid had to say about Poppa and when he was planning on waking up. Momma and Rocket didn't know yet about me and ink and skin and feelings and thoughts and listening, and maybe it wasn't the best time to be telling them, since what I was *not* hearing couldn't be good—couldn't be good at all. Fish and Samson knew. They knew, and they were looking to me to learn what they could.

I shook my head slowly.

Without even a gust or a breeze, Fish turned his back on me and walked out of the room.

"Fish?" Concerned, Momma followed Fish out into the hall, taking Gypsy with her as she left to make sure that Fish was all right. Rocket tried to comfort Samson, but Samson just stood by Poppa's bed like a statue.

It was impossible to believe that an entire room filled with special Beaumont know-how could do nothing to help our poppa. All I could do was listen uselessly. But listen I did. I listened until my ears rang with all the soft beeping and shushing and humming and buzzing of the machines that surrounded him. I listened until my head hurt and my eyes stung with all the tears I was too empty to cry.

Rocket watched me and Samson intently, keeping his eye on us for Momma while she was in the hallway with Fish and Gypsy. Grandpa Bomba dropped into a chair at the foot of Poppa's bed, looking forlorn and older than old.

Then I leaned over Poppa's bed with enormous care and whispered in his ear. "Listen to me now, Poppa. It's time for you to hear *my* voice inside *your* head. You may think you've got no savvy, Poppa, but you're wrong. You do have a savvy. You do." I thought back to everything I knew about Poppa. I thought back to the story of how he'd met and courted Momma, never giving up until she finally agreed to married him, even after Aunt Dinah had told him to shove off. I thought back to the World's Largest Porch Swing and how Poppa always vowed that he'd build us one all our own. I remembered Poppa coming home from work late because he had been determined to pick out the very best special-occasion dress that he could find.

"You do have a savvy, Poppa. You do," I repeated over and over into his ear. "You never give up, Poppa, not ever. That's your savvy. You never, *ever* give up."

I closed my eyes and made a wish, a belated birthday wish in my imagination. I wished that Poppa could hear me. I wished that Poppa would listen. Then I bent down and kissed Poppa's forehead.

". . . give up," said a faint, faint voice inside my head.

I opened my eyes. Samson's hand rested lightly on Poppa's shoulder.

". . . don't . . . give up." The voice came again, a little louder now.

I looked at Samson. I wasn't sure I'd ever seen my little brother cry before, he'd always hidden everything away so well, but he was crying now, making neither a sob nor a sound. The biggest, quietest tears slid down Samson's face to fall and fall like Fish's rain onto Poppa's chest.

Maybe it was Samson, or my words or my wish . . . or a miracle. Or maybe it was the same for Poppa as it had been for my brother's dead pet turtle, maybe nature was only doing what nature does and it was simply Poppa's time to start healing and waking up. We could never really know. Even with a savvy, some things always stay a mystery.

". . . don't give up."

Miss Mermaid shivered and swished her tail ever so slightly, as though the effort was almost too great.

"I don't . . . give up." The voice in my head was louder yet.

"Poppa!" I shouted, certain now that it wasn't just me hoping. The voice came from Poppa and Miss Mermaid. "Poppa, that's right! You don't give up! Can you hear me, Poppa? It's me, Mibs!"

Rocket put his hands on my shoulders and tried to quiet me, but I shook him off. Grandpa rose up out of his chair with a stern look.

"Poppa! Can you hear me? Don't give up!" I shouted again.

"Mibs, stop yelling," said Rocket. "This is a hospital."

"He can hear me, Rocket! I know he can. And I can hear him."

"Mibs, Poppa's not even conscious." Rocket raised his own voice now, sounding tired and vexed. But I ignored him and kept yelling into Poppa's ear.

"Mibs!" shouted Rocket, trying again to pull me away from Poppa.

Without warning, all of Poppa's buzzing, whirring, shushing machines and monitors went berserk. Lights flashed and alarms sounded. Sparks popped from the equipment and the up-and-down rhythm of the line on Poppa's heart monitor went flat with a single terrifying tone.

Rocket turned completely white. A horrified look contorted his face and he began to back out of the room, bumping into Fish and Momma, who had heard all of the commotion and come running. They were followed in by the nurse in the rainbow scrubs.

"Everyone needs to clear this room immediately," said the nurse.

"No!" I shouted. "Poppa needs me! I can hear him!"

"Mibs, please—" said Momma.

I couldn't let them make me leave. I had to stay and listen to Poppa. I had to let him know it was time for him to wake up and that I would be there when he did. I lowered my voice and leaned right up to Poppa's ear again, holding on tight to his bed and ignoring everyone who tried to pull me away.

"You are my good, sweet poppa and it's time for you to wake up and come home. It's time for you to come home and build us that porch swing so that we can sit and think and watch the clouds roll by together. Then I can tell you all about buses and kisses and voices and everything that happened while you were asleep. Don't give up, Poppa. Don't give up!"

More nurses flooded the room and an orderly tried

unsuccessfully to pry my fingers loose from Poppa's bed while a doctor pushed his way through the crowd to check Poppa's heart.

"Mibs?"

"Yes! Poppa! I'm here." I squeezed Poppa's hand. He could hear me. Poppa knew I was there.

"Mibs?"

"I can hear you, Poppa. It's Mibs. It's your little—"

I stopped myself before I could finish saying *little girl*. I didn't feel like a little girl anymore. I wasn't one.

"It's Mibs, Poppa. I'm here."

Poppa's fingers twitched and his eyes fluttered open, making the doctor smile and Momma cry out. Rocket choked on his own tears and Fish whooped and hollered. Feeling Samson's hand in mine, I knew—sure as sure as sure—that everything—*everything*—was going to turn out just fine.

Chapter 37

IT TOOK POPPA A LONG, LONG time to get strong enough to come home to us in Kansaska-Nebransas. Even then, things never did get quite back to the way they'd been before the accident. When something like that comes along, whether it's an accident or a savvy or a very first kiss, life takes a turn and you can't step back. All you can do is keep moving forward and remember what you've learned.

The day I turned fourteen was bright and sunny, a day with nothing more special or important about it than me getting older. Spring was rolling round again and Momma was in the kitchen making my cake. It was the cake I'd wanted so badly exactly one year ago, the cake with the pink and yellow frosting and the perfect sugar roses, the cake that didn't seem quite so very important to me anymore, compared to other things.

Poppa and I were sitting outside on the porch, rocking away on our very own porch swing—the one that Rocket, Fish, Samson, and I had helped Poppa build the previous autumn, even though us kids had undertaken most of it on account of Poppa's head still not always working right. But having a porch swing all our own was something that none of us would give up on either, and we were glad to do it.

Our swing wasn't the World's Largest like the one up in Hebron, nor was it the World's Prettiest. It wasn't even close. But sitting there with Poppa, just thinking and listening as we watched the clouds roll by, I knew our swing was the World's Best. Ours was a real porch swing with a real porch to go with it, and a whole house full of love to hold it up.

Grandpa Bomba slept in a large wicker chair on the

other end of the porch, dreaming of the days when he still had the strength to move mountains, and Fish was sitting on the steps nearby, listening to Gypsy talk to herself as she picked dandelions in the yard with her feet bare and all her clothes on inside out. Fish kept a close eye on our little sister, hollering at her every time she tried to put one of the dandelions in her mouth.

"Cut it out, Gypsy," Fish said, as our sister held a yellow flower to her tongue teasingly. "If you put one more of those weeds in your mouth I'm taking you inside."

"Tell Fish to give us a little push . . ." said a voice inside my head. Miss Mermaid swished her tail as I glanced down at Poppa's arm. When I looked up at Poppa's face, he was rubbing his knuckles against his jaw, smiling. He recognized me that day. That was good.

After coming home from Salina Hope Hospital, Poppa couldn't always remember what day of the week it was or whether or not he liked blueberries in his pancakes. He couldn't recall if we lived in Nebraska or in Kansas and didn't understand that we lived in both, or how that had come to be. On the really bad days he couldn't find the right words for newspaper or coffee or jam or sorry.

But on the good days, the best days—like that spring day on the porch with the smell of baking cakes drifting out to us through the window—Poppa was just Poppa, with no hair on his head to cover up the scars from the accident, but as good and sweet as ever.

"Hey, Fish," I called out. "Poppa and I need a push."

Fish turned his attention away from Gypsy and her dandelions. He screwed up his face for a second and sent a gust of wind that rocked the porch swing hard beneath me and Poppa, almost tipping us right off.

"Whoa! Not so hard!" I laughed.

"Sorry," said Fish with a mischievous grin, giving us another push of wind, a little gentler this time.

With a creak and a bang of the screen door, Momma stepped out onto the porch, her apron perfectly clean, and her cheeks pink from working in the kitchen. She looked around at all of us.

"Where's—?"

"Samson's upstairs," I told her. "He's helping Rocket pack."

"Knowing Samson, he's probably packed himself right into one of Rocket's suitcases," muttered Fish. "No one will find him until Rocket gets up to Uncle Autry's."

Eighteen and free to make his own way, Rocket was catching a bus for Wyoming the very next morning, on his way to spend the summer, or longer, with Momma's brother and his family in a place even closer to the middle of nowhere than Kansaska-Nebransas. On Uncle Autry's ranch, it wouldn't matter how many sparks Rocket unleashed. There was no one around for miles to notice, or care.

Momma and Grandpa had tried to convince Rocket that he was doing fine, that he could scumble his sparks as well as anyone could expect of a young man and that with a bit more work and a few more years he'd have no worries at all. But Rocket had never been quite the same after that day at Salina Hope Hospital one year before. He'd lost his swagger and his bluster. Not once since then had Rocket bragged about his savvy or teased me about my own. He had watched Fish take control of his storms with brotherly pride and quiet envy, but Wyoming would give him the wide-open spaces to work outside and sleep under the stars, giving him room to feel less burdened by his electric savvy.

"How are we going to make the station wagon work without you?" I'd asked Rocket when he'd announced that Uncle Autry had invited him to come and stay.

Rocket had chuckled and popped a few playful sparks. "I s'pose Poppa will have to break down and buy that old tin-can of a clunker a new battery," he said.

It was going to be strange not having Rocket around, especially now that Fish could scumble well enough to start high school in Hebron in the fall. Soon I'd be the only one growing moss in pickle jars and painting pictures with Momma and having school at home. My savvy couldn't harm other people or cause any damage, but Momma and I decided on homeschool anyway, just to be sure.

"A year or two to gain your strength and learn how to scumble your savvy certainly won't hurt you, Mibs," Momma had said. "After that you'll be ready to take on the world."

Momma didn't realize that I'd already taken on the world and won. I'd grown used to all the voices inside of my head and knew which ones to pay attention to and which ones to ignore. The same went for all the voices outside of my head, and this newfound strength must have shown like a mark on my skin, for the next time I ran into Ashley Bing and Emma Flint up in Hebron, those girls kept their mouths shut, without even an echo of a "Missy-pissy" thrown my way.

"Is that boy of yours coming over for the party?" Miss Mermaid asked, breaking into my thoughts about Rocket's departure.

"Yes, Poppa," I answered. "Will's coming over after lunch."

It turned out that neither God nor Miss Rosemary had held my wrong choices against me for too long after all of us kids ran off in that big pink bus. We Beaumonts were back to attending church services with Pastor Meeks and his family, and Will and Bobbi were now regular visitors in Kansaska-Nebransas.

"And that girl . . . ?" Miss Mermaid cut into my thoughts again.

"Bobbi's coming over too, Poppa," I answered with a laugh. "She wants to say good-bye to Rocket before he leaves."

"Hmph," Poppa humphed out loud, and Miss Mermaid snapped her tail. Poppa always pretended that he wasn't fond of Will and Bobbi. I supposed he didn't want to see us kids growing up all around him. But because of Miss Mermaid and because of my savvy, I always heard what Poppa was thinking and I knew that he was glad that we'd made friends—friends who knew all about our family's extra-special know-how and liked us all the same.

With Rocket moving away and Samson and Gypsy still years away from their own most important birthdays, things looked as though they might settle down and stay peaceful for a time. But I knew a secret—a secret that I wasn't supposed to know yet—a secret that might make things get interesting again by winter.

Just because Momma was perfect, that didn't mean she couldn't forget things sometimes. So when she was on the phone with Miss Rosemary earlier in the week, getting the perfect recipe for marshmallow pie, and all she could find was a pen but no paper, Momma forgot about ink and savvies and feelings and listening and she wrote that recipe right onto the back of her hand. She wrote it in pretty red ink. Pretty, *noisy,* red ink.

That was how I found out that Momma was thinking she might be pregnant and that a new little Beaumont was on its way. But that day on the porch swing, that day with its sunshine and its perfect cake, that wasn't a day for spoiling secrets, so I kept my mouth shut and rocked, rocked, rocked in the swing with Poppa.

If only my savvy worked in reverse, I thought again—and not for the last time. If only I could draw a smiling sun on the back of my hand, then everyone around me could know exactly how I felt, exactly how happy I was at that perfect moment.

For just then, things were quiet, and they'd stay quiet for a good long time. At least as good and long as it took Samson to turn thirteen . . .

And who could guess what might happen then?

FIVE YEARS LATER . . .

Samson

(A SAVVY-BIRTHDAY STORY IN TWO PARTS, ABOUT A BOY WHO GETS A TWO-PART SAVVY)

I

"HAPPY BIRTHDAY, SAMSON!" Mibs peeked her head into my room. "How are things going up here? Feeling okay? Anything out of the ordinary happening yet?"

My bedroom was dim despite the bright slits of noontime sunlight trying to force their way through my closed blinds. I'd been sitting in my beanbag chair all morning, alone in my darkened room, munching potato chips and reading, trying not to think too hard about the fact that today was my thirteenth birthday. Trying not to dwell on the knowledge that, by day's end, I'd likely feel utterly different than I felt yesterday. *Savvy* different.

"Did Momma send you to check on me?" I grumbled, sorry my words sounded lower and more growly than I'd meant them to. I twitched my older sister an apologetic grimace.

"You know she did." Mibs chuckled, beaming encouragement at me. I couldn't help but smile. At nineteen, Mibs's encouragement still felt as comforting as it had when she was twelve and I was seven, when she would help me up the steep steps of the school bus every morning, assuring me that everything would be okay, even though the other kids always teased us.

"Can I have one of those?" She nodded toward my chips.

Leaning forward, I held out the entire bag, the crackle of the packaging warring with the noisy scrunch of my beanbag chair.

Why did so many awesome things also have to be so loud?

A distant crunch-a-munch of car wheels churning up our family's long dirt and gravel driveway made us both turn our heads. Mibs took the bag from me, popped a chip into her mouth, and then offered me a small silent wave as she went to see who was arriving. She took the potato chips with her.

I hesitated a moment, listening to the approaching car. Then I jammed a scrap of paper between the rumpled library pages of *The Invisible Man*, by H. G. Wells, and laid the book down on the floor.

Who could be arriving now? Neither Poppa nor Momma had gone out that morning; my parents wouldn't have left our property for anything. Not today.

On the other side of my bedroom door, it was all hands on deck getting the house ready for me to turn thirteen. Momma and Gypsy were busy wrapping all the breakables in bubble wrap. Fish was packing up every sharp object he laid eyes on. Poppa stood in the backyard contemplating whether or not to board up the windows.

Even Grandpa Bomba was helping out. Last I'd seen him, Grandpa was sitting in a lawn chair next to the house, a blanket draped over his lap. He had been flinging dirt this way and that with a wobbly flick of three knobby fingers, using his savvy to dig a narrow trench, in case the family needed a place to shelter outside.

My youngest brother, Tucker, meanwhile, was sitting in the hallway just outside my bedroom door, securing his many hand-me-down toys—metal cars, plastic dolls and action figures, even a few of his stuffed animals—to the floor using wads and wads of beige masking tape. Just in case.

No one ever knows what to expect on a savvy birthday, so it's best to be prepared for anything.

All morning, I'd been trying to prepare the only way I knew how, conserving my energy—and my sanity—in the manner that best suited me, finding a quiet spot where I could be alone. A difficult task when you're from a big family.

It wasn't that I didn't like people; I did, particularly the people in *my* big family. I just felt better equipped to handle my anxiety about getting a savvy of my own . . . well, on my own. Momma told me there was nothing wrong with that. Poppa assured me we'd keep my birthday party one hundred percent mellow and low-key.

"We don't even have to sing 'Happy Birthday,' Samson," he'd told me, "if it makes you feel too scratchy. I know how you hate being the center of attention, kiddo."

As the sound of the car drew closer, I raked my hair back from my face and climbed out of my slouchy chair.

Had Rocket changed his mind about coming down from Wyoming? I hoped so. I understood why my electric brother felt happier—and less hazardous—living at our uncle's ranch, in one of the least densely populated places in the country.

But I still missed him. I was glad both Fish and Mibs had returned home for my big day, even if I didn't like being in the spotlight or having a fuss made over me.

These days, Kansaska-Nebransas ought to have been three times quieter with half of the Beaumont kids grown up and moved away. And truly, home would have been peaceful if it had only been Gypsy and me living with Momma, Poppa, and old Grandpa Bomba. But four-year-old Tucker easily made up for my long clammed-up silences and the hours Gypsy spent in a state of day-dreamy preoccupation.

"Hey, everyone! Someone's here!" Tucker's voice rang through the house as the car in the driveway killed its engine and three car doors opened and slammed closed in quick succession: *Bang! Bang! Bang!* The sounds echoed alongside the loud *thump, thump, thump* of Tucker's small feet as he barreled down the stairs.

Muffled voices filled the air outside, and the doorbell rang—again and again and again—like someone was leaning on it. I flinched at the ruckus, feeling a headache sprouting between my molars.

Curious to know who was on our porch, I slipped out of my bedroom and moved past my little brother's cluttered installation of tape and toys. I stopped at the top of the stairs, lingering there like a ghost. Or a tall, thin stretch of shadow.

Momma's voice drifted up to me from the entryway. "Oh! Why . . . Dinah! You didn't tell me you were planning to visit with the kids. And today of all days! Did you three drive here? All the way from Indiana?"

"We wanted to surprise you," my aunt's voice replied.

"There hasn't been a savvy birthday in the family in quite some time. Not since Mibs turned thirteen! And with my Ledger next in line for his a few years from now, I thought it would be good for him and his little sister to share their cousin's special day. Won't Samson be delighted to see Ledge and Fedora? The more the merrier, right?"

"Well . . . actually," Momma measured her words with perfect care. "You know we're always glad to see you, but I've mentioned before how Samson prefers *smaller* gatherings."

"Oh, piffle! Tell me you're happy we came, Jenny!"

"*I'm happy you came*, Dinah." Momma's reply was automatic. A little too automatic. Even from the top of the stairs I could tell she'd only said the words because she'd had to. Aunt Dinah's savvy gave her the ability to rob people of their free will whenever and however it suited her. It made me feel sorry for my cousins. I hoped my new savvy didn't make me as bossy and controlling as their mom was.

It wasn't long before the entire family had converged in the entryway below me, greeting the new arrivals. Gypsy whisked Ledger away to the dining room, insisting he help blow up balloons. And Tucker and Fedora raced up the stairs and then past me, each holding tight to a thick new spool of masking tape.

"Don't worry, Mibs," Dinah said as she hugged my sister. "I made sure the kids didn't have a single jot of ink or marker anywhere on them before we got here. I don't want you to have a brain full of tater tots and tinker toys, or whatever else my children think about on a daily basis."

"Thanks, Aunt Dinah." Mibs laughed, clearly relieved.

"And you!" Dinah gave Fish a squeeze too. "Working for a television weather channel now? Really? Isn't that a bit on the nose, young Mister Twister?" Before my brother could answer, Dinah gave him a sly smile and added, "Your mother also tells me you're in love. And with a young woman from another savvy family, too! Why, there are so many more of us than I'd ever realized. Later, I'm going to make you tell me all the details!"

Fish may have been twenty years old, but his face went maroon with embarrassment—and horror. A gust of savvy-powered wind whistled around him, blowing over Momma's leafy Ficus and rattling all the crepe paper streamers Gypsy had hung earlier. Poppa shot Fish a sympathetic look, sharing an eye-roll with him behind Aunt Dinah's back.

Wishing to avoid Aunt Dinah as long as I possibly could, I slipped back into my bedroom until the others vacated the entryway. Then I grabbed *The Invisible Man*, as well as two more books, three comics, and an old National Geographic magazine.

I was sneaking downstairs, headed for the door—hoping to make it all the way to the nylon camping hammock strung between two trees in the backyard—when I heard another set of tires in the drive.

Could *that* be Rocket's truck?

My heart sank as the doorbell rang again. Rocket wouldn't ring the bell; he'd walk right in.

"Must be someone's birthday!" the mailman observed as I opened the door with Gypsy twirling past behind me waving a blue balloon.

I nodded to the mailman, but my gaze was drawn up the road, toward yet another approaching vehicle. A green and yellow delivery truck from a flower shop in Hebron.

"Blast it all!" swore the mailman. "That truck is going to block me in if I don't get a move on." He loaded me up with a stack of cards and packages—too many to fit in our mailbox at the end of the road—balancing them atop my armful of books and comics. He then quickly turned to go.

Only, he wasn't quick enough. The floral truck had already parked behind him.

As if the driveway weren't already crowded enough, an aging gold minivan came bumping up the road. I recognized the van right away; it belonged to our pastor and his wife. I was struck by a sudden panicked thought:

Had I gotten my savvy without realizing it? Had I turned into a people magnet? Would more and more relatives and strangers continue to arrive, until I was suffocated by a bevy of brash voices and birthday hugs? Terror corkscrewed through me. Momma and Poppa had taught me the word *introvert* before I could spell my own name, explaining that some people need a hefty dose of alone time to recharge their batteries, to store up the fortitude they need to give their best to others and the world. But I was sure I was downright demophobic. I learned that word on my own. It means: *afraid of crowds*.

I began to sweat and shake as the driveway filled with cars and people. The mailman had begun to argue with the driver of the floral truck. There was a loud *POP!* as the van—with our pastor's wife, Miss Rosemary, behind the wheel—shimmied in the gravel and came to a sideways stop across the road, brought to a standstill by a blown-out tire.

It looked like no one would be leaving Kansaska-Nebransas anytime soon.

"What's all this then, Samson?" Grandpa Bomba brushed dirt off his sleeve as he hobbled slowly up the front steps and settled himself into his rocker on the porch, looking out at the scene in front of us. Before I could answer, Tucker burst through the open door behind me looking like half a mummy; Fedora had bound him elbows-to-neck in masking tape. She chased after him, brandishing her roll of tape. Saying, "Don't run away, Tucker! You said you *wanted* to play spider tag. I caught you fair and square. Now I get to wrap you up like a bug." Fedora began shouting, "Wrap! You! Up!" over and over at the top of her lungs, waving her tape.

"Help, Samson! Help!" Tucker ran rings around me, Fedora on his heels. Grabbing the edge of my tee shirt, my brother wound it *tight, tight, tighter* around my chest and stomach as he circled me. I stood in place, holding my teetering armful of books and parcels high. It wasn't long before Gypsy and Ledge came to see what was happening and quickly joined in the chase: Gypsy laughing as she ran interference for Tucker; Ledger growling as he tried unsuccessfully to take the tape from Fedora.

I began to feel weak and thin. Practically transparent.

"Helloooo!" Miss Rosemary called from the driveway as she climbed out of her van. She clutched a Bible and a giftwrapped present in one arm, her purse and a large bowl of ambrosia salad in the other. "Hello, everyone! Helloooo! I've come with gifts and prayers for the birthday boy! But it looks like someone's going to have to change this tire for me."

It was time to hide.

As the rest of the adults spilled from the house onto the porch, and the mayhem in the driveway grew to a frenzied pitch, I couldn't take another second of the chaos. My head pounded. My knees had become taffy. I squeezed my eyes closed, feeling everything go fuzzy. Until . . .

"Whooooa."

I opened my eyes again and saw that my cousin, Ledger, had stopped short. He stood rooted in place, his eyes wide and darting all around the spot where I was standing. Ledge's face had lost its color. His mouth hung open.

"Wait!" shouted Tucker, halting in his tracks as well. "Where did Samson go?" Then my little brother did the most extraordinary thing. The most terrifying thing.

He ran straight through me.

II

IF IT HADN'T FELT SO STRANGE, I probably would have noticed sooner how I'd begun to feel . . . *better*. My headache was gone. My muscles had relaxed. My hands—

I looked down at my hands and became immediately disoriented.

My hands were *gone*. So were all the books and packages whose textures and weight I could still feel. Looking down, I saw the scuffed wooden porch boards beneath my feet. Literally beneath my feet. Because my feet were now invisible, and, apparently, incorporeal. When Fedora began to madly wave her roll of tape through my middle, stepping closer to where she'd seen me standing a moment earlier, she should have hit me in the gut. She should have stepped on my toes. But she didn't.

What had happened to my toes?

Had I died on my feet without realizing it and promptly become a ghost?

Totally freaked, I let go of everything I was holding. Books and packages spilled everywhere, becoming visible to me and everyone else again the moment they hit the ground. Momma and Poppa both shouted my name as *The Invisible Man* thumped down in front of them.

"Samson? Samson!"

Then Fedora tripped over one of the boxes and fell through my legs. Smacking her chin against splintery porch boards, she began to shriek the way only five-year-old girls can shriek.

Soon everyone was shouting: "Fedora!" or "Samson!" or "What happened?" or "Where are you?"

No one could see me. No one but—

"What's wrong, Momma?" Gypsy looked from me to Momma, then at all the others who were calling out my name. Even the mailman and the delivery driver were staring searchingly in my direction, mouths ajar. And Miss Rosemary had stiffened, pulling her lips into a tight, disapproving pucker. The pastor's wife had never grown entirely accustomed to the outlandish things that occurred whenever we Beaumonts were involved.

"What's the matter, everyone?" Gypsy raised her voice over the din. "Samson is right there." She pointed at me. "He *has* gone a little"—my sister cocked her head and squinted—"a little *airy*. A little flimsy-filmy. But I can totally see his eyelashes and edges. Oh! Samson!" Gypsy's eyes went wide when she finally realized that something very peculiar had indeed happened to me—something that could only be explained by one thing: My savvy. My very own thirteenth-birthday talent. A talent I'd have to learn to control and live with for the rest of my life.

I had no idea why Gypsy could see me when no one else could. But my little sister had always had a way of seeing things other people overlooked. Things other people couldn't see.

She rushed toward me. "What's happening to you, Samson?"

I should have said something. I should have let my family help me. Instead, I fled. I wanted nothing more than to find an itty-bitty hiding spot somewhere, where I could fold myself up tight, catch my breath, and figure out exactly what *was* happening to me.

It's a catawampus, collywobbly sensation to be both invisible and incorporeal. To be a living ghost. It was like I'd vanished from existence entirely, except for the fact that I could still see and think. I could still smell the manure in our neighbor's cow pasture. I could still taste the salt from my last potato chip in the corners of my mouth when I nervously licked my lips. I could still hear the buzz and snap of grasshopper wings. The warbling songs of the meadowlarks.

It was as if I was both in the world and not in it, at the same time. I could barely register the warmth of the sun on my skin or the sensation of grass beneath my shoes as I sped in the direction of the backyard hammock, which I hoped to wrap myself up in for the next . . . well, *forever*.

What I could feel though was a peculiar surge of strength and power charging up inside me. Charging like a battery. It began in my toes, a slow-building supply of palpable energy, ready for . . . ready for . . . what exactly? I didn't know.

Somehow, I got myself snugged up tight inside the hammock without falling through it or turning *it* invisible. I knew there were likely rules to this new talent of mine, things about my new savvy I'd have to learn. But just then, all I wanted to do was pull the sides of the hammock up and around myself and rock awhile between the two tall trees that held it up—while attempting to figure out exactly how to reappear. What if I couldn't? What if I were stuck like this forever?

It was Gypsy who told Fish and Mibs where to find me. Though, I immediately wished she hadn't, because that's when things grew seriously out of control.

"Don't worry, Samson. It's just me and Fish and Mibs," Gypsy said, leaning in close to whisper in my ear.

"Are you in there, Samson?" Fish tapped his knuckles uncertainly against the side of the hammock. "I know you usually prefer to sort things out alone, but we're all worried about you."

I could feel Fish's worry. It came at me in small bursts of wind that gently rocked the hammock. And a low cloud moved in to hover over the backyard, threatening rain.

"Just tell us you're okay, Samson," Mibs implored.

I couldn't decide if I wanted to shout "Go away!" or beg my brother and sisters to sit with me until I figured out how to make myself turn back to normal. But Gypsy, Fish, and Mibs had already decided what they were going to do. When I peeked out from inside the hammock, they were all still there, each with a steadfast hand resting on the hammock. Unwavering devotion sat fixed on all their features. Clearly, none of them planned to leave my side anytime soon.

Any irritation I might have felt melted into desperate waves of gratitude. I reached out, hovering my right hand directly overtop Fish's wrist, not wanting my fingers to drop all the way through his and make my stomach fall with them. I was startled when a buzzy sensation began to zigzag between the creases in my palm, and patches of my hand began to materialize again, if only for a moment. A knuckle. A fingernail. A freckle.

My brow furrowed. What had made *that* happen?

I lightly touched the tip of my pinkie to Mibs's index finger. The same zig-zaggy feeling shivered around the spirals of my fingerprint.

It was something I'd done a hundred times before, lightly touching someone's arm or hand as a way to connect, or as a way to shore another person up when they were feeling low. But this time it felt different. This time, I felt as though every bit of energy that had begun to charge up inside me the moment I turned invisible was now flowing into Fish and Mibs. The longer I stayed in contact with them, the more visible and solid I became, until—in my excitement to feel more myself again—I flipped over in the hammock and face-planted hard into the grass.

I didn't mean to trigger any of the things that happened next. My impossible birthday talents were still fresh out of the box. I didn't know yet that my new savvy made me into a virtual battery: something hidden from the eye that supplied power to other things.

Seeing bits and pieces of me beginning to reappear, both Fish and Mibs bent to try to help me off the ground. I rolled over and reached for them. But this time, when I clamped my hands around their shoulders, things began to happen. Powerful things.

Fish reeled back. As he did, the wind picked up, strong enough to straighten Gypsy's curls and make her hug the nearest tree. The shelf of clouds above us turned into a swirling black-and-green anvil. The sky flashed with heat lightning.

With a cry, Mibs bent double, her hands pressed tightly over her ears. At first I thought she was reacting to Fish's sudden earsplitting booms of savvy thunder, but I quickly realized she was trying to block out an altogether different onslaught of noise. Noise only she could hear. I could just make out her words as she groaned, "Ahhh! It sounds like I have the thoughts of everyone from here to New York City inside my head. Samson! What did you do?"

"Samson?"

I pulled myself up, spun around—and smacked right into Rocket.

Rocket! My eldest brother had come home to help me

celebrate after all. Only, the damage was done the moment I pressed a hand against his chest.

The buzz that zigzagged from my fingertips hit my electric brother with the power of a premium-grade commercial generator.

"Oof!" He stumbled backward a few steps, his hair standing on end. When he straightened up, blue filaments of electricity lit his eyes, and then crackled out from every part of him, sizzling in high-frequency, high-voltage alternating currents.

The snaking tendrils of blue light immediately developed a positively charged channel between the earth and Fish's storm clouds. Bringing down the lightning.

Several bright jagged bolts struck the fields around us. Another hit one of the trees holding up the hammock—the tree opposite the one Gypsy was hugging—blackening it and splitting its trunk in two. Gypsy shrieked and ran back toward the house to take cover, even as Momma, Poppa, Grandpa Bomba, and the mailman came running into the backyard to see what was happening. As soon as the mailman did see, his eyes went round and he jumped into the trench Grandpa had dug earlier. I pictured Miss Rosemary tossing her bowl of ambrosia salad into the air and diving back into her van to take cover. Aunt Dinah must have ordered my cousins into the house at the first sign of trouble; I could see Ledge goggling out at us through the kitchen window.

So far, it had been an eventful day. I'd turned invisible, which had made me feel better and stronger, like there was an energy source deep inside of me that was charging up;

then I'd somehow made my brothers' and sister's savvies more powerful than they'd ever been. Just by touching them.

Drained from such a sudden and intense transfer of strength, I stood in the middle of the pandemonium, almost entirely visible and corporeal again. Visible and corporeal and dizzy and embarrassed and . . . wet. Water dripped from my hair into my eyes, and stuck my tee shirt to my chest. Fish's storm cloud had given way, and it had begun to pour down rain.

I wanted to shout, "I'm sorry! I'm awful. I didn't mean to do any of this!" But as soon as the thoughts passed through my mind, Mibs lowered her hands from her ears and grabbed me, wrapping me tight inside a hug.

"You are *not* awful, Samson," she said. "You could never be awful. None of this is your fault, even if it might feel like it is. You couldn't help it. But you'll learn how to. Trust me. And trust yourself."

At first, I tried to pull away, scared I would only make things worse for Mibs the longer she held onto me. But my sister refused to let go, and I soon found myself shaking against her shoulder, trying not to cry.

The surge of power I'd heaped upon my brothers and sister did not last long. Fish's storm, Rocket's fluxing blue volts of electricity, the thousands of ink-less voices inside Mibs's head—the thoughts and feelings of people near and far—they all subsided almost as quickly as they'd begun, leaving all of us exhausted and—

"Ready for cake?"

Grandpa Bomba saluted me as he called across the yard

in his creaky voice. "Whooo-eee! Is this a birthday party, or is this a *birthday party*?" And slowly, slowly, we all trooped inside. Though Poppa stayed back just long enough to help the mailman climb back out of the hole in the ground.

I felt like a wrung-out dishtowel by the time I stepped back inside the house. But while everyone else headed for the dining room, ready for lunch and cake and presents, and still marveling loudly over my new talents, I stopped short at the bottom of the stairs, thinking I heard someone crying.

I turned left instead of right and stepped into the family room. Five-year-old Fedora sat on the floor in front of the sofa, knees drawn tightly to her chest. Sniffing and blubbering, she pressed a bag of frozen peas against her chin. When she shifted the bag, I glimpsed the scrapes and bruise she'd gotten when she fell through me on the porch.

"Can I sit by you, Fe?" I asked her quietly, pointing to the carpet next to her. I still felt shaken by everything that had just happened, but I could see my little cousin was hurting.

Fedora nodded and began to cry harder. Yet through her tears, she stammered, "Did you . . . did you get your savvy, Samson?"

"Yeah," I said, sitting down and drawing my knees up to my chest, too. "Yeah, I suppose I did."

"And it makes you"—*sniff*—"it makes you turn invisible?"

My voice wobbled. "It . . . it seems to do a little more than that."

Fedora looked up at me, her eyes red and puffy. She hiccupped. "What else does it do?"

"Maybe . . . maybe I could show you." I reached out a

hand, thumb up, fingers half-curled, concentrating with all my might on trying to scumble my new savvy.

"Thumb war?" I challenged her, quirking a half-smile. But Fedora only shook her head, lips quivering, tears still rolling down her cheeks.

"My chin hurts."

"Come on, Fe," I urged her gently. "One game. I'll even let you win." With another sniff, Fedora reached out with her free hand. As we clasped fingers, a single remaining zigzag of energy flowed from my hand into my cousin's.

Fedora stopped crying. She put down her frozen peas and grinned at me, feeling better. Feeling stronger. Ten-times stronger, I guessed, than she'd felt the moment before. Somehow, this small triumph made me feel better.

I grinned back at her.

It was a start.

DISCUSSION QUESTIONS

- Describe Mibs and her unique family. Would you want to be part of the Beaumont clan or not? Why?

- Describe Mibs's relationship with her parents and siblings. How is it complicated by their savvies? Do you think the inheritance of a savvy is a curse or a blessing? Why? What have you inherited from your family?

- *Savvy* is told in the first person; how would the story be different if someone besides Mibs were telling it? Do you think changing the point of view would make the story better or worse? Why?

- Why is Lill Kiteley's arrival such an important one for Lester? In what ways is she able to help him change and grow as a person? Predict what the future will be like for the couple.

- How does Mibs's relationship with Will and Bobbi change over the course of the adventure? Who do you think changes the most in the story? Why?

- Momma warned Mibs that "you can't get rid of part of what makes you you and be happy." What can we infer from Momma's statement? Do you agree with her? Provide some examples from the story to validate her point.

- Using the phrase, "This is a story about . . . " supply five words to describe *Savvy*. Explain your choices.

- When Bobbi talks to Mibs about Will's obvious feelings for her, Mibs realizes that it "made me feel too young and too old at the same time." Why does she feel this way? Have you ever felt this way? How does Mibs deal with these feelings? How do you?

- Mibs considers, "Maybe it's like that for everyone, I thought. Maybe we all have other people's voices running higgledy-piggledy through our heads all the time. . . . I began to realize how hard it was to separate out all the voices to hear the single, strong one that came just from me." What can readers infer about her statement?

- Mibs thinks, "Then I remembered what Lill had said just before falling asleep in the motel the night before. You never can tell when a bad thing might make a good thing happen. I realized that good and bad were always there and always mixed up in a tangle." In what ways is this statement an indicator of Mibs's growth?

Turn the page for a preview
of the next book about
the Beaumont family—

Chapter 1

MOM AND DAD HAD KNOWN ABOUT the wedding at my uncle Autry's ranch for months. But with the date set a mere ten days after my thirteenth birthday, my family's RSVP had remained solidly unconfirmed until the last possible wait-and-see moment. We had to wait until my birthday came and went. We had to see if anything exploded, caught fire, or flooded before committing to a long-haul trip across four states in the minivan. In my family, thirteenth birthdays were like time bombs, with no burning fuse or beeping countdown to tell you when to plug your ears, duck, brace yourself, or turn tail and get the hay bales out of Dodge.

I'd known for years that something in my blood and guts and brains and bones was poised to turn me tall-tale, gollywhopper weird. On my thirteenth birthday, a mysterious ancestral force would hit like lightning, giving me my very own off-the-wall talent. My very own *savvy*. Making me just like the rest of the spectacular square pegs I was related to.

My mom's side of the family had always been more than a little different. I doubted there were many people with a time-hopping great-aunt, a grandpa who shaped mountains and valleys out of land once pancake-flat, and a mix of cousins who ranged from electric to mind-reading to done-gone vanished—*Poof!* I'd even had a great-uncle who could spit hailstones like watermelon seeds, or gargle water into vapor and blow it out his ears. When Great-uncle Ferris turned thirteen, his savvy had stunned him with a sudden, sunny-colored snowstorm inside the family outhouse, toppling the small shack like an overburdened ice chest that rolled down the hill with him still inside it.

As for me, I'd been sure my birthday would treat me

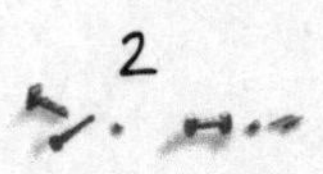

better—sure I had the perfect mix of genes to make me supersonically swift. Unlike Mom, Dad was ordinary, but even without a savvy, he was still one of the best runners in Vanderburgh County. So it was practically destiny that I'd become the fastest member of the Theodore Roosevelt Middle School track team. The fastest kid on the *planet*.

Nothing worked out the way I'd hoped.

On my thirteenth birthday, I didn't get bigger, better, stronger muscles, or start racing at the speed of light. I didn't get the ability to whiz blizzards in the blaze of summer, either. But it wasn't like I hadn't gotten a savvy of my own.

Watches and windshield wipers everywhere, look out! I could blow stuff apart without a touch, dismantling small things in bursts of parts and pieces: a light switch here, a doorknob there, garage door opener, can opener, Dad's stop watch, his electric nose-hair trimmer too. After the first few episodes, I shoved whatever I couldn't fix underneath my bed. I didn't want Mom and Dad to know how much stuff I was breaking. Already,

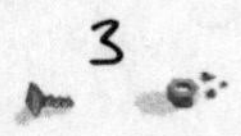

I could see my future: No more training with Dad for the father-son half marathon in the fall. No track team, no more school, no friends. Rather than flinging crinkle-cut dills in the cafeteria, I'd be staying home to grow moss in pickle jars like my Beaumont cousins. Because if I hit Josh and Ryan and Big Mouth Brody Sandoval with ceiling panels and table hardware instead of handfuls of baby gherkins, Josh and Ryan might laugh it off, but Big Mouth Brody would tell for sure—and that wouldn't go over well at home.

Family rules said *keep quiet*. No one risked the consequences of sharing the family secret unless they had to; it was impossible to know what might happen if people found out that we weren't normal. Nicer folks might want to hire us for our skills. Less nice ones might want to put us in a freak show, or lock us up to study us and try to decode our genomes.

Well, secrecy was fine by me. The ability to bust apart a toaster wasn't something I cared to boast about. It helped that Dad was clearly in denial, while Mom believed she had everything under control. As far as

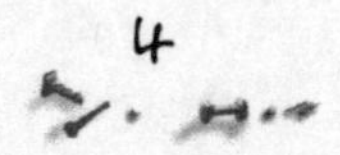

my parents were concerned, I was simply Ledger Kale, doohickey-destructo boy less-than extraordinaire. And I was happy to let them think it.

So, nine days after I turned thirteen, Mom and Dad confirmed our family's RSVP and we packed our bags, preparing to hightail our way west from Indiana to Wyoming.

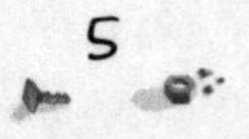

Turn the page for a glimpse at the whimsical and wonderfully moving companion book—

Chapter 1

"PLEASE, MRS. FOSTER—I'VE SEEN your future, and you really don't want to buy this soap."

"Gypsy Beaumont! Stop making a scene and *let go*."

It was the second Saturday in January, but red and green streamers still hung from the rafters in Flint's Market. A little drummer boy continued to *rum-pum* over the loudspeakers. At the front of the store, a small table held what was left of the holiday clearance: mesh bags of crushed chocolate Hanukkah coins; flattened marshmallow Santas; a torn package of silver confetti; a few scraggly, wilted poinsettias. Meanwhile, halfway down aisle six, I was engaged in a tug-of-war with Mrs. Foster, my former Prairie Scout troop leader and the mother of my *former* best friend, Shelby.

As Mrs. Foster and I battled for possession of a small blue box of Suds o' Heaven bath soap, Shelby pushed her mother's grocery cart down the aisle, away from us. Pretending she didn't know me.

Just like she'd been doing for the past four months.

"What happened to the good citizenship you learned in Prairie Scouts, Gypsy?" Mrs. Foster demanded.

"I'm trying to be a good citizen," I said, wrenching down harder on the box Mrs. Foster and I gripped between us.

Mrs. Foster didn't understand. Couldn't understand. She only tugged back harder. "I never could get you to conform to the conduct of the Prairie Scouts, Gypsy. You were always too flighty."

Yank. Tug.

"Too daydreamy."

Jerk. Pull.

"Too . . . too *odd*. Where are your parents?" Mrs. Foster pried at my clutching fingers, not letting go of the bar of soap that was, unbeknownst to her, as dangerous as an oily banana peel at the top of a staircase.

Hearing Mrs. Foster's voice rise over the post-holiday

rum-pa-pum-pums, I knew I was in trouble. By now, Poppa would have heard the shrieking. He'd be hotfooting it to aisle six, on the double. Mr. Flint would probably be heading our way too. The store owner always kept a close eye on my family when we did our shopping. Things had a way of going wonky when a Beaumont was in the aisles—from exploding cash registers and power surges, to an incident involving all of the ink pens and markers in aisle ten, to an unexplained rainstorm in the bakery that destroyed a dozen birthday cakes and gullywashed fifty loaves of bread into the parking lot.

Mr. Flint had already banned most of my older siblings from the store, for life.

It looked like I'd be next.

I hadn't meant to make a scene. Seeing Shelby and her mother in the store, I'd followed them, slipping away from Poppa in the produce section. When I'd left him, Poppa had been scratching the old scar on his bald head as he sorted through a pile of fresh green beans, trying to pick the perfect ones for Momma. Momma could've grabbed handfuls of the very best beans without even looking, but today Poppa had volunteered to do the shopping. I'd asked to go along. Big mistake.

I'd followed Shelby, spying on her from a distance. I was certain that, if I looked hard enough, I might glimpse a future in which I was a super-mature, card-carrying teenager in Shelby's new gaggle of gawking, squawking gal-pals.

No such luck. I'd seen Mrs. Foster's future instead.

I could feel my glasses slipping down the short slope of my stubby nose. Not wanting to release my two-handed grip on the soap, I used my shoulder to push my glasses back in place. It was either that or close my eyes, and keep them closed. Otherwise things would only get worse.

If Poppa arrived in aisle six now, he'd know I'd been using my *savvy* again. I was supposed to be practicing control. I was supposed to be staying focused on the present. I was supposed to be allowing other people their privacy . . .

But I'd never been too good at remembering my *supposed-to*'s.

"Gypsy!" Poppa appeared at one end of the aisle, just as Mr. Flint materialized at the other. Both of them were frowning. At the same moment, the music inside the market changed. The drummer boy's plodding *pums* faded away, replaced by a lively burst of violins and horns and spritely tambourine: the Russian Dance from *The Nutcracker*. Hearing the familiar melody, my mind filled with a fantasia of dancing thistle-men and orchid women. Lifting my spirits. Compelling my feet to move.

The zeal of the music, and the threat of the three adults closing ranks, bolstered my determination. With one great heave, I snatched the soap from Mrs. Foster's grasp at last. I lingered just long enough to plow every last bar of Suds o' Heaven off the shelf, into my arms. Then I sprang merrily away.

"Gypsy, stop!"

"I can't, Poppa," I called back. "Trust me!" Hop-skipping down aisle six, I hugged my hoard of soap tightly. I couldn't afford to drop any of the slippery boxes; I had to keep them all from Mrs. Foster.

Overtaken by orchestral glee, I only paused when I passed Shelby.

"Come on, Shel. Please?" I begged as I twirled and

hopped around her. "You could help me." All I wanted was to skip away arm-in-arm with Shelby, to giggle and cavort the way we'd done less than a year ago, when we were both still Prairie Scouts, and friends.

Shelby stared at the floor, bug-eyed and red-faced. Completely mortified.

I felt my shoulders droop. But I couldn't dawdle. Mrs. Foster's future was in my hands.